Eureka:

The Life of Edgar Allan Poe

A Novel

by

Sara Wilburn

To Brian, Tesla and Mila, for being my family.

To Edgar Allan Poe for the lifetime of joy, fascination, comfort, entertainment and inspiration that your life and work have given to me and to the world.

"To the few who love me and whom I love - to those who feel rather than to those who think - to the dreamers and those who put faith in dreams as in the only realities - I offer this Book of Truths, not in its character of Truth-Teller, but for the Beauty that abounds in its Truth; constituting it true. To these I present the composition as an Art-Product alone : let us say as a Romance ; or, if I be not urging too lofty a claim, as a Poem.

What I here propound is true: — therefore it cannot die: — or if by any means it be now trodden down so that it die, it will 'rise again to the Life Everlasting.'

Nevertheless it is as a Poem only that I wish this work to be judged after I am dead."

- Edgar Allan Poe, *Eureka*, 1848

On a worn bed covered in faded linens shone the bright red hair of a beautiful woman. Her rosy cheeks gave the impression of robust health, but the pallor of the rest of her face and the sweat of an intense fever revealed the truth. Two little boys, just toddlers, played with toy trains on a nearby rug, mercifully too young to understand what was happening. In the arms of a well-dressed lady, a baby howled inconsolably, as if she were the only one present who fully understood. Two younger women looked on, wringing their hands and exchanging pained glances, as if they wanted to help, but had no idea what to do.

The dying woman weakly coughed and a rivulet of blood trickled out of her mouth. One of the ladies, grateful for something to do, knelt down and gently wiped it away with a lace-trimmed handkerchief, murmuring words of comfort. The other knelt down and spoke to the youngest boy.

"Edgar, dear," she said, gently touching the boy's cheek, "I need you to do something for me. I need you to go over to your mama and tell her that you love her."

Happy to oblige the pretty lady, he smiled and toddled over to the bed. He laid his head down on his mother's chest and did his best to wrap his tiny arms around her. She drew in a sharp, rattling breath and began coughing violently, blood gushing from her mouth. The lady dove into action, quickly scooping up the boy and shielding his face from the horror. The sounds were terrible as Eliza Poe, a beautiful and talented actress of only twenty-four, drowned in her own blood. Little Edgar craned his neck to see her, his grey eyes wide, as Fanny Allan held him more closely, knowing that she must be his mother now.

Little Edgar reached his arm up to hold Fanny Allan's hand as he stood on the Richmond docks with her, his doting foster mother, and John Allan, his reluctant foster father.

"I want to see Henry and my baby sister before we go," chirped Edgar.

"She's at least half your sister, anyway," snorted John, exhaling tobacco smoke.

"JOHN!" Fanny shot him a reproachful look as John laughed and returned to smoking, pleased with himself.

Edgar didn't know exactly what had just happened, but he knew he'd been insulted somehow and frowned. Fanny knelt down, straightened his collar and his hair, smiled at him and kissed his cheek.

"I'm afraid there's no time to see Henry and Rosalie right now, but once we get to England, you can write them as often as you like!" she said.

Edgar fought back tears but ultimately the excitement and fascination of the journey ahead and the massive, awesome ship that would take them there trumped the sadness of missing his siblings.

It was time to board. John and Fanny ushered him directly to their cabin, much to Edgar's irritation, as he wanted to stay on deck and watch the sailors. He sighed, lied down on one of the berths and grabbed a favorite storybook. A few pages in, his missed naptime overtook him and he fell asleep.

Throughout the grueling, 45-day voyage, John smoked, drank scotch and obsessively planned every detail of the England branch of Ellis & Allan and was generally unavailable. This suited Edgar just fine. Less fine was the fact that Fanny was also generally unavailable, as she was incapacitated by seasickness. This would have made for a lonely, boring voyage for the average boy, but not for Edgar. He explored the ship freely, small enough to fit anywhere and examine all the nooks and crannies. He befriended all the sailors, who seemed to view the large-eyed, curly-haired, precociously articulate little lad as something of a mascot. He earned the nickname "Ned" and they answered his many questions, teaching him the names of all the parts of the ship. By day, he loved to stare out onto the horizon, looking for land or for ships, hoping to spot a whale. By night, he snuck up onto the deck with John Allan's portable telescope and gazed at the moon and the stars. When they arrived in England, he considered stowing away, he was so sad to leave his sailor friends and the total freedom he'd enjoyed… especially when he learned that he'd be attending boarding school in Stoke-Newington while the rest of the family stayed in London.

England struck Edgar as grey, green and damp.

Everything was covered in moss from the perpetual clouds

and rain. He missed Richmond's sunshine and he missed

Fanny and her sweet voice, soothing hugs and the fantastic

snacks she made him. There were no hugs at boarding

school, that was for sure. Only cold, ultra-formal Doctor

Bransby who seemed to have no actual personality, save

the empty façade of strict, harsh headmaster. Edgar was

bored stiff; all the schoolwork was easy for him. He

breezed through it, finishing early, which left him with

nothing to do but daydream, staring out the window, or

composing semi-naughty limericks about Doctor Bransby

for the amusement of himself and his classmates. He spent

a lot of time sitting in the corner and a lot of time clapping erasers outside, simultaneously getting rained on while inhaling chalk dust.

In time, he got used to it, and made quite a few friends. Doctor Bransby even grew on him. That man seemed to know everything, and occasionally would give little Edgar a wink or a smile of approval. Doctor Bransby would never admit it out loud, but he secretly admired the little boy's pluck, creativity and spirit. Just when Edgar had really settled in, however, he was yanked out of school. The England branch of Ellis & Allan had collapsed and the family was returning home in ruin.

Back in Richmond, the family lived for a while in the tiny apartment above Ellis & Allan. It was cramped and annoying and Fanny cried constantly. She had come from aristocracy and this was not the life she'd expected. She loved her husband and she loved her boy, though, so she put on a brave face whenever possible. "We have food and we have shelter… technically," she thought, gritting her teeth. "I should be grateful." Edgar saw how miserable she was, so he never complained and did his best to make her laugh.

During this period, Allan drank a lot more scotch than usual. This made him even more impatient and even quicker to anger than usual, and for Allan, Edgar became the scapegoat for everything that was wrong in the family and in the world. Edgar was therefore subject to many an unnecessary, undeserved thrashing and Edgar learned to dodge Allan as much as was possible in such close quarters. He learned to stay in bed and quietly read when he wasn't playing outside.

Thanks to Ellis & Allan's selection of imported books, Edgar had plenty of excellent reading material, much of which he'd learned to love during his time in England. He adored the sarcastic reviews and horror tales of *Blackwood's Edinburgh Magazine*. But just when he'd settled into a nice rhythm of playing outside all day and reading in bed by candlelight all night, news arrived of the death of Allan's mind-bogglingly rich uncle, William Galt. The struggle was over. The Allan family was rich.

Edgar worked part-time as a clerk at Ellis & Allan when not at school or practicing maneuvers for the Richmond Junior Volunteers. His financial problems permanently solved, Allan's drinking had quieted way down and thus so had his rage toward Edgar, and this was mostly a time of peace. When General Lafayette came to Richmond and Edgar's regiment led the parade, escorting the esteemed general through the streets, Allan beamed, telling Edgar for the first time that he was proud of him. At the store and on the streets of the parade, Edgar repeatedly noticed one very pretty girl who was obviously also noticing him. Eventually, he got up the guts to ask her out. Her name was Elmira.

Edgar ran with two schoolmates down the banks of the James River, which roared and foamed after a series of summer thunderstorms. The air was thick with humidity and smelled of rain and earth. The boys laughed and joked as they ran.

At the water, Edgar stripped off his shirt and fearlessly dove in. He knew he was a strong swimmer, that this wild current was nothing for him, and he was sure that he would win the bet. He would swim all the way to Warwick against the current with no problem. The other two boys followed, albeit less confidently.

They swam, performing an ill-advised physical feat in a show of bravado of which only young boys are capable.

Elmira had tried to dissuade Edgar from attempting this.
She had asked him if he was sure it was worth risking his
life to win a bet. He answered as any young man would,
"Aw, it's nothing." He thought of her as he swam. He used
the image of her flawless skin, her bright blue eyes, her
supple curves as motivation to push onward when he
started to get tired. His heart pounded and his muscles
ached, but the water felt good, and the promise of victory
and impressing his girlfriend felt even better. He pushed
onward, far ahead of his mates, all the way to the dock at
Warwick, the finish line. There waiting for him was Elmira,
her hands partially covering her eyes, as if she couldn't
bear to watch. Edgar climbed out of the water and grinned
triumphantly.

"Oh, Edgar!" yelled Elmira. "Your back! It's as red as a
lobster's!"

Edgar walked to his dorm, laden with books, from the newly-founded University of Virginia's half-finished library. The university was still under construction and in only its second session. Edgar entered the front door of his dorm and carried his books past mayhem – boys passed out on the stairs, drunken laughter, carousing. The hallway was a mess, festooned with crumpled paper and broken furniture. He arrived at his room – room 13 – and went inside, breathing a sigh of relief. This small and minimally-appointed room was his sanctuary.

The room contained only a bed, a small table and a firewood rack, on which only two logs remained. Edgar put his books down on the table, grabbed Voltaire from the stack, and settled in for a read.

He contentedly read and as the sun began to go down, started to doze when a loud crash followed by angry yelling snapped him awake.

"Goddammit," he swore.

A full-on fistfight had broken out directly outside his door. Again. He rolled his eyes in irritation and tried to continue reading when two boys crashed through the door, landing on the floor, the one boy on top of the other, throwing punch after punch, breaking the other boy's nose. Blood cascaded down the boy's face and onto his shirt.

"Get out of here!" yelled Edgar. "What the hell is wrong with you?!"

The boys looked at him in disbelief, snapped out of the oblivion of their drunken fight, as if they wondered what he was doing there. He shoved them bodily out the door and attempted to close it behind him, only to discover that it wouldn't shut.

"Shit," he muttered.

He used one piece of firewood to make shims to close the door and threw the other in the fireplace to make a small, pathetic fire. It was February, and now that the sun had gone down, it was cold.

He read by candlelight, concentrating as well as was possible under these irritating conditions, with the horror and shock of the bloody fight he'd witnessed intruding constantly on his thoughts. He forged on like this for a while, not really retaining anything, until a loud party across the hall made it impossible to concentrate. He sighed and checked his front pocket. Two dollars. With

resignation, he closed his book and headed across the hall.

The door to the room across the hall hung wide open.

The beds had been shoved against the wall and the room

had been converted into a makeshift casino. Drunk boys

and two trashy girls played cards and caterwauled. Wadded

dollar bills were piled high. Edgar hesitated for a moment

before deciding to enter. He had nothing better to do.

He sauntered up to the card table.

"Got room for another?" he asked, the Southern accent

he'd acquired in his last few years back in the states

popping through.

Wordlessly, the dealer pushed out a chair with his foot

and nodded.

As dawn began to break, only Edgar and the dealer were still conscious. All the other boys and both girls were passed out in heaps. Edgar smiled, yawned and contentedly accepted a $10 bill from the chagrined dealer. He stood up and headed back to his room to catch an hour or two of sleep before the day's classes.

Subsequent gambling sessions didn't go so well. Edgar was in some pretty deep shit. Tired and stressed out, he walked to the campus post office. There waiting for him was a letter from John Allan. Edgar excitedly, hopefully tore it open and to his immense relief, there was a $50 bill inside.

Edgar headed back to his dorm, relieved and happy to pay his debt off. This would cost him $35, which would leave him $15 for living expenses. He was saved.

He entered the Den of Iniquity, as it had come to be known, and confidently walked up to the dealer.

"Poe. Here to settle up?" sneered the dealer.

"Yes. I hope you have change for a $50," Edgar replied.

"No change. You owe $50," the dealer snarled.

"What?! No! I owe $35!" stammered Edgar.

"Haven't you been paying attention in math class?" laughed the dealer. "Interest is a bitch."

Edgar stared at him in disbelief and turned several possible scenarios over in his head before relenting and handing the $50 over. He glared pure hatred at the dealer. This was a setback he didn't need, but he knew how he'd handle it. "I'll win it all back and then some tonight, you son of a bitch," Edgar thought.

As dawn broke over the cold, half-constructed campus, groups of boys, for once sober and dressed in their Sunday best, picked up trash and decorated the campus for a special family visit day. It looked half-assed, cobbled-together and downright silly, but the young men did the best they could.

Edgar sat on the steps of his dorm, nervously tapping his foot, his eyes darting around. From around a corner, John Allan appeared, and Edgar sprang up, happy to see the only father he'd ever known.

As Allan approached, he coldly, robotically stuck his hand out for a handshake as Edgar reached to hug him before quickly, awkwardly realizing that no hug was intended and settling for the handshake. His cheeks burned with embarrassment.

"Nice to see you, boy!" grinned Allan. "What are you waiting for? Give me the official tour."

Edgar, still a bit stung by Allan's cold greeting, nodded and led the way.

Edgar sat on the bed, watching Allan slowly pace as he surveyed Edgar's dorm room, cataloguing its contents.

"Why don't you have a chair?" Allan asked.

"I haven't been able to afford one yet," answered Edgar.

Allan snorted.

"You're only enrolled in two classes. I thought you were going to take three," said Allan, his voice dripping with contempt.

Edgar, getting irritated, replied, "You only gave me enough money to enroll in two."

"What the hell are you talking about?" demanded Allan. "I gave you a hundred–ten dollars."

"Yes, and I needed a hundred-fifty even to take the two classes that I'm taking! I've had to go to humiliating lengths to make up the difference," explained Edgar, raising his voice.

"I repeat, what the *hell* are you talking about?" Allan yelled back.

"Cards," Edgar sheepishly answered. "I had to resort to gambling. I… owe three-hundred dollars."

"Pathetic," seethed Allan. "But what could I have expected from the son of an *actress*."

Edgar was damned tired of Allan taking shots at his mother. He leaped up and got in Allan's face.

"Don't you ever say a *word* about my mother," Edgar growled.

Allan grunted and smiled contemptuously, but this didn't shake Edgar one bit.

"While we're on the topic of mothers," continued Edgar, "congratulations on the birth of your *twins*. It must be a miracle. I thought ma was barren."

Allan's face fell as if he'd been slapped. How could Edgar know about this? He moved closer, so that the two men's faces were almost touching.

"You son of a… You keep your nose out of my affairs," snarled Allan.

"'*Affairs*' would be the correct term, wouldn't it?" Edgar shot back.

For a moment, it appeared that they would come to blows, but finally, Allan stepped back and started for the door. Edgar sat down hard on his bed, dejected by this utter failure of a father-son visit.

"Before you go," Edgar stammered, fighting back tears, shaking with adrenaline. "Have you seen or heard from Elmira?"

"I have seen her, actually…" smiled Allan satanically. "I've seen her all about town with her new beau." With that, he turned and left. Edgar stared slack-jawed out the door after him.

Lying on his side in bed, Edgar wrote by the dim light thrown by candles that stood on the windowsill. The firewood rack held pieces of the table that he used to use for writing and two of its legs fueled an anemic fire. He seemed unaware of these squalid conditions, however, as he passionately, rapturously wrote "Tamerlane."

"My passions, from that hapless hour,
Usurp'd a tyranny, which men
Have deem'd, since I have reach'd to power
My innate nature — be it so:
But, father, there liv'd one who, then —
Then, in my boyhood, when their fire
Burn'd with a still intenser glow;
(For passion must with youth expire)

Ev'n *then*, who deem'd this iron heart -

In woman's weakness had a part.

I have no words, alas! to tell

The lovliness of loving well!

Nor would I dare attempt to trace

The breathing beauty of a face,

Which ev'n to *my* impassion'd mind,

Leaves not its memory behind.

In spring of life have ye ne'er dwelt

Some object of delight upon,

With steadfast eye, till ye have felt

The earth reel — and the vision gone?

And I have held to mem'ry's eye

One object — and but one — until

Its very form hath pass'd me by,

But left its influence with me still." **(1)**

He poured out his emotions in a torrent: regret, sadness, futility, anger, loss and love.

"We grew in age, and love together,

Roaming the forest and the wild;

My breast her shield in wintry weather,

And when the friendly sunshine smil'd

And she would mark the op'ning skies,

I saw no Heav'n, but in her eyes —

Ev'n childhood knows the human heart;

For when, in sunshine and in smiles,

From all our little cares apart,

Laughing at her half silly wiles,

I'd throw me on her throbbing breast,

And pour my spirit out in tears,

She'd look up in my wilder'd eye —

There was no need to speak the rest —

No need to quiet her kind fears —

She did not ask the reason why.

The hallow'd mem'ry of those years

Comes o'er me in these lonely hours,

And, with sweet lovliness, appears

As perfume of strange summer flow'rs;

Of flow'rs which we have known before

In infancy, which seen, recall

To mind — not flow'rs alone — but more

Our earthly life, and love — and all." **(1)**

Today he had lost more than his beloved fiancée,

however. He had also lost his home. There was no way he

could return to Richmond, not now. John Allan had made it

clear to him that there was nothing for him there. He was

on his own. He had to find his own way, find somewhere

else to go.

"I reach'd my home — my home no more —

For all was flown that made it so —

I pass'd from out its mossy door,

In vacant idleness of woe.

There met me on its threshold stone

A mountain hunter, I had known

In childhood but he knew me not.

Something he spoke of the old cot:

It had seen better days, he said;

There rose a fountain once, and *there*

Full many a fair flow'r rais'd its head:

But she who rear'd them was long dead,

And in such follies had no part,

What was there left me *now*? despair —

A kingdom for a broken — heart." **(1)**

Wiping tears from his eyes with his sleeve, he set his

new poem aside and headed across the hall.

Inside the Den of Iniquity, the usual melee raged. Boys drank and fought. One boy, in a stupor, fingered a pistol. Edgar ordered a drink from the shoddy old table that served as a bar.

"Shot of whiskey."

The bartender slammed a sizeable shot down on the table. Edgar drank it down in one gulp, stifling a grimace at its bitterness.

The alcohol flooded his sensitive system, unaccustomed to alcohol's effects. He surveyed the room. He watched the boy with the pistol pass out, heard the thud of the gun hitting the floor. His heart pounded. The sounds of the room were dull, as if his ears had been stuffed with cotton.

Fortified, he sauntered over to the card table, intent on

giving the dealer a piece of his mind. But as he reached the

table, his eyes widened. He clapped his hand over his

mouth and bolted frantically out of the room as the others

laughed.

Feeling the effects of last night, a prematurely haggard Edgar emerged from his French class. Slowly, he moved down the hallway to a bulletin board around which was gathered a small crowd of boys who hooted victory or swore defeat. He pushed his way in toward the bulletin board. There he saw his grades: Edgar Allan Poe, 3rd in class in Latin and 6th in French. His mouth curved slightly into a satisfied smile.

Despite having his first hangover, there was a spring in his step as he walked to the library. As he headed between two buildings, the card dealer popped out from behind a pillar and began to follow him. Edgar noticed this and quickened his step. The card dealer quickened his step, too,

and Edgar broke into a full run.

Edgar, hungry and thin, clad in an Army uniform, carried his manuscript, "Tamerlane and Other Poems," through the streets of Boston. He reached a door marked "CALVIN F.S. THOMAS, PRINTER" and entered.

Moments later, he emerged and continued walking to the harbor where he boarded a ship bound for Sullivan's Island, South Carolina. The nametag of his uniform read "Pvt. Edgar A. Perry."

The Army quickly realized that Edgar had a multitude of talents that it could put to use. His fine, analytical mind, ability to concentrate, attention to detail and communication skills got him the coveted job of clerk, meticulously keeping Fort Moultrie's records. After serving with distinction as a clerk for a while, he gained the officers' trust and was promoted to the important and potentially dangerous job of artificer.

"Day after day, day after day, we stuck, nor breath, nor motion," Edgar stood at a desk covered in formulae and calculations in the artificer's shed, reciting "The Rime of the Ancient Mariner" from memory, gingerly pouring gunpowder into a bomb.

"As idle as a painted ship, upon a painted ocean," bellowed a friend, entering the shed and startling the shit out of Edgar.

"GodDAMN it, Charles," Edgar breathed, his heart pounding, thankful that he had finished pouring gunpowder a split second before his friend had entered.

"Ha ha! Sorry, Poe, I couldn't resist," laughed Charles. "I just came by to bring you your mail."

"Oh, thanks," grinned Edgar, regaining his composure.

"Anytime," grinned Charles, strutting out the door.

Edgar smiled after him as he opened his letter. The instant he began to read, his face fell.

Wearing his Army uniform and carrying a heavy trunk, Edgar walked with a military rectitude down the Richmond street on which stood the Allan mansion. Reaching the mansion, he breathed a sigh of dread, gathered his strength and knocked on the door.

The butler opened the door and gestured Edgar in. Edgar entered, looking around, marveling at the grandeur of it. He entered the study, where Allan sat facing the window in an armchair, gazing vacantly out at the street.

"Pa…" said Edgar, "I'm so sorry. I got here as quickly as I could."

Allan slowly turned around, flinching slightly when he saw Edgar, taken aback by the strong, confident gentleman who stood before him.

Allan cleared his throat. "You missed her funeral. It was yesterday."

Edgar hung his head. "I'm sorry. I was hoping to get here in time."

"It was sudden," said Allan limply.

"I loved her as I would have loved my own mother," said Edgar.

"I know you did," replied Allan, his voice breaking.

He took a moment to collect himself and to admire the impressive young man that Edgar had become. His amazement at the change in Edgar bubbled over and forced to comment, he stood up and approached Edgar.

"Look at you. Who ever would have expected this…
this *man* standing before me!" gushed Allan.

Edgar smiled, taking in this rare compliment. Allan turned to look out the window as he continued talking.

"Your creditors from Charlottesville are still dunning me, you know," snorted Allan.

"I'm sorry," Edgar sheepishly replied.

"Well, at least you excelled at *something* at the university," said Allan, jovially but with an audible layer of resentment.

Edgar snorted an uncomfortable laugh.

Allan turned to face Edgar and became earnest for a moment. "I'm sorry I ignored your letters."

Edgar nodded. Allan startled him by approaching, placing his hand on the back of Edgar's neck and laughing in disbelief, admiring Edgar's chiseled, manly face.

"I hope you'll join me for dinner," said Allan.

From opposite ends of a long dining table, Edgar and John Allan conversed as the maid cleared away the plates and silverware. Allan leaned his chin on his hands, his elbows tented, mulling something over, as Edgar excitedly told Allan of his wishes and plans.

"I've already risen as high as I can in the Army. I've gotten all I can from it in a year and a half. Were I to complete my five-year term, I'd be wasting the prime of my life," explained Edgar.

Allan, visibly not delighted, continued to skeptically listen.

"If you could use your influence to get me a cadet appointment at West Point, I could one day become an officer. I could get the education I need to rise to a position of public eminence, which is what you raised me to want."

Allan mused for a moment, rubbing his chin.

"I'll write some letters," Allan replied. "I can't promise anything."

"Of course! Thank you, that's all I ask," Edgar grinned.

"It won't happen overnight," said Allan. "This might take some time."

Edgar, with a trunk at his feet and another in his arms, awkwardly knocked at the door of a small, no-frills, red brick Baltimore row house. He waited, nervously looking around, until the door opened and a tall, big-boned woman emerged, wearing a widow's cap, her face bearing the premature signs of aging of a difficult life. She smiled warmly at him, and in that smile, he could see that she had once been very beautiful.

"You must be Edgar," she smiled.

"Aunt Maria," he smiled back.

She moved aside to let him in, holding the door for him.

He stepped inside the sparsely furnished but tidy house. Everything was second hand or worn, but mended and kept in impeccable condition. These were impoverished but proud people. As Edgar set his luggage down, an adorable, ethereally beautiful little girl strutted into the room, curious to meet her cousin. She had put on her best dress for the occasion – faded and slightly too big, but it made her feel pretty nonetheless. She smiled and curtsied.

"Hello, Edgar. I'm Virginia," she said.

"It's *so* nice to meet you, Virginia," Edgar replied, laughing joyfully at her sheer cuteness and her precocious confidence and self-assuredness.

She instantly liked her handsome cousin and blushing, she ran giggling back into the other room to return to playing with her dolls.

"She's a bit shy," said Maria, misreading her daughter's sudden exit, "but she'll warm up to you. Let me show you the rest of the house."

Maria led him down the hall to a back bedroom.

"Now, he's been very ill and I'm not sure you two would even remember each other, you were separated at such a young age," she whispered.

Edgar's eyes widened. Could it really be? He waited nervously as Maria quietly opened the door and poked her head inside the room.

"Henry?" she said gently, "You'll never guess who's here."

She gestured Edgar inside. Propped up on pillows, pale and covered in sweat, with a half-empty bottle of gin next to him lied Henry Poe, Edgar's brother. Though he last saw him when both were toddlers, Edgar recognized him immediately. Edgar fought back tears, so shocked and happy he was to see his brother. He ran to the bed and threw his arms around him.

"Henry!" he cried.

Henry coughed. Edgar looked up to see blood trickle down Henry's chin. Edgar watched helplessly, bewildered and horrified. He looked to his aunt for some kind of explanation, though he already knew exactly what this meant. Maria gently pulled Edgar away and led him out of the room, quietly shutting the door behind them.

"He became ill a couple months ago. The gin is certainly not helping, but he's in so much pain…" She swallowed hard. She had been dreading the moment she'd have to deliver this news to Edgar. "He's been unable to work for weeks, and we're in the last extremity…"

Edgar solemnly nodded.

"You're welcome to stay, though," she continued. "You can earn your keep by tutoring little Virginia."

"Of course! I'd be delighted. Thank you, Aunt Maria," he breathed, processing this bittersweet welcome.

"Please, call me 'Muddy.' Everyone does," she smiled, shaking her head. She patted him on the shoulder and headed for the kitchen. Edgar smiled, happy to be living among blood kin for the first time since his mother died, despite the difficult circumstances.

Edgar shared Henry's room, and despite Henry's severe illness, the brothers enjoyed trading stories and getting reacquainted when Henry felt up to it. Henry had been a sailor for several years before he became ill, and he'd seen all sorts of action. Some of it Edgar was sure Henry had made up for his amusement, but he played along and pretended to believe it all as gospel. They talked about beautiful girls, teenage exploits and epic pranks, condensing into a short time an entire childhood that they wished they could have shared. Edgar didn't remember his mother at all, and was grateful to hear the few memories of her that Henry, being a year older, was able to recall.

When not getting reacquainted with Henry, Edgar tutored Virginia in English and math at the kitchen table. She was a bright pupil, though she shared her cousin's subversive bent and love of humor. She hated math and her reward for paying attention, not whining and trying hard was a new joke at the end of each session. She never let her cousin forget this daily tradition, triumphantly slamming the book shut and asking excitedly, "Is it time for today's joke?"

"Hmmm," Edgar pretended to muse, rubbing his chin, "I suppose it is."

Virginia raptly waited, giggling in anticipation, as Edgar looked around the room for inspiration.

Finding it, he turned to her. "Why might a regular rowdy be eaten?"**(2)** he asked.

Virginia frowned, pondering. She shook her head and replied, "I don't know."

"Because he's a loafer bred," Edgar said, confidently delivering the punchline.

Virginia frowned again, not getting it. Edgar reached over and popped open the breadbox. She got the joke, bursting with laughter, yelling, "A loaf of bread!"

His laughter trailing off, Edgar said, "You've been doing so well with your schoolwork, Sissy. I got you a little something."

"Like what?!" replied Virginia, nearly leaping out of her chair with childish excitement.

From behind his back, Edgar produced a simple, sweet ragdoll. With wide eyes, Virginia gratefully plucked it from his hands and threw her arms around him. "Thank you,

Eddy! I love it!" she squealed.

Eventually John Allan's half-hearted letter-writing campaign bore fruit and Edgar received word that he was to report to West Point to begin his education as a cadet.

Edgar didn't want to leave his family. He had grown to love them all very much and had just, for the first time in his life, truly begun to feel at home; to feel a sense of belonging. The family was living hand-to-mouth, though, wretchedly poor with absolutely no prospect of any future improvement unless Edgar, the only able-bodied male, could find a way to make a good living. Becoming an officer in the Army would do it, he thought, so with a heavy heart he forced himself to go.

He stood outside the family's row house with Muddy, wraith-like Henry, and little Virginia, who tightly clutched her doll and valiantly fought back tears.

"I'll write as soon as I get to West Point," Edgar said, doing his best to conceal the fact that his voice was shaking. "I'm going to miss you all terribly."

He knelt down to talk to Virginia. "I'm going to miss *you* in particular, Sissy."

She bit her lip and a single tear rolled down her cheek from her brimming eyes. Edgar gently wiped it away and kissed her cheek as she barely held in a sob. He smoothed her hair and placed his hand on the side of her head, looking directly into her eyes.

"You just practice your arithmetic and I'll be back to visit before you know it," he whispered, his own eyes brimming.

She nodded, unable to talk, lest she burst into tears.

Reluctantly, he started down the sidewalk, laden with two trunks. He turned and glanced back at Virginia, who mustered a wistful smile and a little wave.

Edgar's body ached from the day's field training exercises and maneuvers. His stomach growled. Supper was never quite enough to replace what had been burned off by the day's exertions. Bored out of his mind, he stared out the window at a gorgeous pink-orange winter sunset as Sergeant Locke, his nemesis, taught a stultifying evening class. Edgar stifled a yawn, took note of the clock ("Thirty bloody minutes to go," he thought) and returned to memories of evenings spent with his family. He was fully elsewhere, deep within a reverie of after-supper hilarity with Sissy and Henry as Muddy cleaned the kitchen and looked on, shaking her head in disbelief at the raucous silliness she was witnessing. The house was warm and still permeated by the scent of a truly impressive beef stew. Sigh… heaven. The bell rang, startling him out of his daydream but releasing him from the torturous imprisonment of the classroom.

At 10:00 PM Edgar returned to the barracks, his entire being looking forward to how good it would feel to lie down. He kicked off his shoes, grabbed an issue of *Blackwood's* that he kept hidden in a pocket of his cloak, lit a candle and dead-tired, settled in for a read. He'd been waiting for this moment all day. He was so tired, unfortunately, that he only got half a page in before he began to doze and the terrible Sergeant Locke snatched the book from his hand and cruelly blew out his candle.

"What's this trash?" Locke scoffed, examining the magazine. "Regulation number five states that no cadet may possess any literature unrelated to his studies."

Edgar seethed, shooting Locke a face-melting dirty

look, but bit his tongue. He rolled over, pulled his blanket

over his shoulders and went to sleep.

The next morning, the detested alarm went off at 5:30 AM. As all the other cadets scurried to get into their uniforms and out to the mess hall, Edgar groaned and pulled his blanket over his head. He stayed there, waiting for silence. He lied there in the dark, staring up at the ceiling, his mind working rapidly as he turned over various ideas for ways to get himself out of this mess. He ached for home. He missed his brother and hoped he was alright. He missed sweet Sissy and her heartwarming giggles. He missed Muddy's soft voice and kind words of maternal guidance. He missed the sense of belonging he felt there in Baltimore, a feeling he had never felt before.

As the sun rose, he hit upon a solution. Grinning, he rolled over, dug a copy of *The Edinburgh Review* out of his cloak, fluffed his pillow and cracked open the book.

He read all morning. He thought it was one of the best days of his life. He stopped only to go to the mess hall for lunch, where his fellow cadets stared at him, some in disbelief, others in admiration. After filling up on hot buttered rolls and milk, he walked back to the barracks, got back into bed and continued reading, alternately smiling, frowning and scrawling notes in the margins. He went on for a few days like this until finally, he received a notice to report to court – his plan had worked.

Edgar was thrown out of West Point for Gross Neglect of Duty and Disobedience of Orders. He got to keep his uniform cloak, though, which kept him warm as he happily walked from the train station to Muddy's house, back home in Baltimore.

He dropped his trunk on the front steps and knocked, shivering both from the cold and from the excited anticipation of seeing his family again. Muddy opened the door, her face reddened from crying, a handkerchief pressed to her face.

"Muddy… what's happened?" Edgar stammered, shocked.

"Henry…" Muddy wailed in reply.

She opened the door to let him in. Leaving his trunk on the porch, he bolted inside and down the hall to find Henry's white corpse lying on the bed, covered in a linen shroud. Edgar gasped, devastated, his eyes filling with tears.

Edgar, now the family's sole breadwinner aside from the little bit that Muddy was able to bring in as a seamstress, read all day and wrote all night. He sent his manuscripts to every journal and newspaper that he could find. Nervously, he walked to the post office every day, hoping and waiting for some good news, for success in any degree. As he leafed through the day's mail, his heart nearly stopped. There was a letter from John P. Kennedy, Esq. of Baltimore's *Saturday Visiter.* He tore it open and read it as fast as he could. "YES!!" he yelled, startling the other post office patrons. He smiled apologetically, turned on his heel and ran home.

He burst through the front door, frightening Virginia, who dropped her knitting.

"I won!" he breathed. "I won the contest!"

"What contest?" demanded Muddy.

"The Saturday Visiter… held a short story contest… I entered… and I've won the contest and *fifty dollars!"* he panted.

Virginia and Muddy, sharing a look of relief and joy, threw their arms around him, cheering for him, proud of him and filled with hope.

Muddy's lifetime of poverty had taught her to truly stretch a dollar, and that fifty dollars meant that life was good for a little while. She chopped carrots and onions, dropping them into a steaming pot of stew as Edgar tutored Virginia at the kitchen table.

"Eddy, I *hate* diagramming sentences," complained Virginia.

"I know, dear, but it's the best way to understand grammar," replied Edgar, gently but firmly.

Virginia sighed.

"Draw a line for the preposition here," he continued, pointing to the paper. "Which word is the preposition?"

"'Of'?" Virginia answered, tentatively.

"Excellent!" said Edgar. "Now write it on that little line."

As Virginia leaned over to write, her hair cascaded onto the paper. Edgar swept it up and behind her ear, tracing her ear lovingly, in a sweet, tender gesture. Virginia smiled at him adoringly. They gazed into each other's eyes for several moments until Edgar, being a gentleman, realized what was happening and looked away. Muddy, having paused her vegetable chopping, saw it too, and was less than delighted.

Even with masterful scrimping and penny-pinching, fifty dollars doesn't last forever and the family soon returned to hand-to-mouth existence. Edgar wrote and wrote and mailed manuscripts left and right. He even worked occasionally as a day-laborer, laying bricks for a pittance.

He sat at the kitchen table staring at the glowing coals of the fire, his chin balanced on his hands, frowning, his mind churning and turning over, grasping at straws of ideas for what to do next.

Muddy entered with the day's mail and placed a letter before him.

"From Richmond," she said, ominously.

Edgar snatched it up, quickly tore it open and read to the bottom. He rolled his eyes and turned away, slapping the letter onto the table, crossing his arms and fighting back tears. Muddy picked the letter up and quickly scanned it before uttering an oath and walking over to stare out the window.

Her voice shaking, she swore, "Mr. Allan left you NOTHING?!"

"Nothing," replied Edgar, in a mixture of disbelief and resignation. He hadn't wanted to believe that Allan would do this, but he had half-expected it.

"But…" stammered Muddy, "He adopted you…"

"No, never formally," replied Edgar. "And he has *many* biological children to provide for."

Though Edgar had half-anticipated it, this was a major blow. Part of him had counted on an inheritance from John Allan's wealthy estate, even though he knew that it was stupid to do so. Now even the shade of a possibility was gone. There would be no windfall, no rescue, not even the slightest possibility of a way out, of a sudden reversal of his family's hardscrabble, impoverished existence. This loss of all hope rendered Edgar despondent, along with the full, total, sweeping and final rejection that came with it. This was cold, hard evidence that Allan had really never given a shit about him, and that hurt.

Sitting on the front porch of the house the family barely held onto month to month, he cried, gazing at the stars, combing them for some kind of answer.

Suddenly, a bright shooting star whooshed by. Edgar gasped, staring wide-eyed at the sky, hoping for more. Seconds later, two more came, lighting the sky up as brightly as daylight. He bolted inside the house, moments later returning with a sleep-addled, nightgown-clad, complaining Virginia. All complaints ceased when she saw why he had woken her. She turned to him, smiling in gratitude that he thought to share this wonder with her. She wrapped her arms around him for warmth and they watched the sky together in awe.

At the kitchen table, Edgar, Virginia and Muddy ate a meager supper consisting of a few potatoes and a scrawny chicken that Muddy had managed to get on credit. All the shelves and cupboards were empty, as were their pockets.

Edgar cleared his throat.

"I have some news," he said.

"Oh?" asked Muddy.

"As you know, I haven't been able to find anything approaching steady work here in Baltimore," he continued.

Virginia frowned, fearful of what was coming.

"I want to provide for the both of you, and in order to do so, I need work… so I've accepted a job in Richmond, as editor of the *Southern Literary Messenger*," he explained, closely and nervously watching Virginia's face as he spoke.

"That's wonderful!" exclaimed Muddy.

Virginia stood bolt upright, her chair screeching against the floorboards, and sobbing, she ran all the way to her room and slammed the door.

Edgar, upset at having wounded his dear cousin, got up, tossing his napkin onto the table, and ran after her.

He could hear her crying through the door. He knocked and poked his head into the room.

"Sis…"

"GO AWAY!" she screamed, her face buried in her pillow.

Edgar walked quietly over to the bed, sat down and stroked Virginia's hair.

"Sissy…" he cooed gently, as she continued to wail, "I'm not leaving you and Muddy… You ran away before I could finish. As soon as I get settled in Richmond and find a nice place for us all to live, I'm going to send for you and Muddy."

Virginia rolled over and looked at him, her eyes red, her face tear-stained, her nose snotty.

"What?" she stammered.

"You don't mind moving to Richmond, do you?" Edgar smiled.

Virginia's face lit up and she threw her arms around him, burying her face in his shoulder.

"Of course not!" she cried, "I'll go anywhere with you!"

His last night in Baltimore, Edgar lied in bed, gazing out the window of the tiny attic that served as his bedroom. Filled with simultaneous anticipation and trepidation, he couldn't sleep. As he began to doze, soft footsteps on the stairs woke him. There at the foot of the bed stood Sissy in her white nightgown, her long hair sparkling in the moonlight.

"I can't sleep," she whispered, her voice giving away the fact that she'd been crying.

"Neither can I," Edgar replied. He reached out his arms toward her.

She went to him, getting under the blanket, wrapping her arms tightly around him. She nestled her head into his chest. He smiled, breathing in the scent of her hair as he kissed the top of her head. Wrapped together, they fell asleep.

Before an ornate desk sat Edgar. Behind it, sat T.W.
White, the owner of the Southern Literary Messenger.
Much more a businessman than a man of letters, T.W.
briefed Edgar on the magazine's goals and operations
before handing him the reins.

"I think you're fully capable," said T.W. "But I
question your judgment and I'll tell you why."

"Please, do tell," replied young, eager Edgar.

"This tale of yours, 'Berenice.' I don't think it's what
my readers want to read. It's bloody and horrifying! Pulling
teeth from a woman who's risen from her grave?
Disgusting!" scoffed T.W.

"I probably shouldn't have sent that tale as an example of my abilities," Edgar explained. "I wrote it on a bet that I couldn't write an effective tale on so awful a subject."

"I presume you won," chuckled T.W.

Edgar nodded. "I can't imagine I'll ever write anything that gory again."

"Good," T.W. agreed.

"But if you want your journal to be popular, you'll have to have an open mind about such subjects. Some of today's most popular articles are in a similar vein. Look at any issue of 'Blackwood's,'" Edgar confidently continued.

"I'd give my left arm to have half of Blackwood's circulation," said T.W., leaning across the desk toward Edgar.

"Then trust me," Edgar smiled. "I won't lead you wrong."

T.W. leaned back in his chair, lacing his fingers over his considerable belly, sizing up the confident, energetic young gentleman that sat before him.

Exhausted by a hard day's work at his new job, Edgar trudged into his basic hotel room, kicked off his shoes and flopped onto the bed. He leafed through his mail, tossing unimportant letters aside until he encountered one from Muddy. He smiled and sat up, happy to hear from his family. With gleeful anticipation, he tore the letter open.

As he read, his smile quickly became a frown. He sat bolt upright, panicked.

"Cousin Neilson has offered to take Virginia into his home, where he could better provide for her and prepare her for entry into society," wrote Muddy. "She'd be given a formal education and would then attend finishing school, which would greatly improve her prospects for marriage. What do you think? What should I tell him?"

His heart pounding, he stood up and paced around the room. He stopped, staring out the window. Still holding the letter, his shoulders heaved as he hung his head and sobbed.

He dashed to the desk, grabbed writing paper, threw himself into the chair and began writing.

"My Dearest Aunty,

I am blinded with tears while writing this letter – I have no wish to live another hour. Amid sorrow and the deepest anxiety your letter reached me – and you well know how little I am able to bear up under the pressure of grief – My bitterest enemy would pity me could he now read my heart – My last my last my only hold on life is cruelly torn away – I have no desire to live and *will not...*" he wrote, as tears fell onto the page, causing the ink to run. **(3)**

That's all of his letter that he could finish for now. He wiped his tears away with his sleeves, stood up, threw on his cloak and left, slamming the door.

Fighting tears, he walked, the cold night air freezing his tear-stained cheeks. Seeing a bar, he strode in and ordered a drink.

He looked like such a mess, the other bar patrons left him alone as he drank. Sufficiently numb, he threw some cash on the bar and left with a drunken swagger.

The next morning, he stumbled, unshaven and disheveled, into work. He tried to concentrate on his editing but could not. He set his pen down and stared at the wall with bloodshot eyes. He felt powerless to do anything to alleviate his heartbreak. He knew Virginia would be more secure with cousin Neilson… she might even be happy. How could he tell her "Don't go?" But at the same time, the idea of losing her made him lose all will to live, all will to do anything.

He finished his letter to Muddy, "Adieu my dear aunty. I cannot advise you. Ask Virginia. Leave it to her. Let me have, under her own hand, a letter, bidding me good bye — forever — and I may die — my heart will break — but I will say no more." **(3)**

He chewed on the end of the pen for a moment, thinking, before adding a note to Virginia in the postscript.

"For Virginia,

My love, my own sweetest Sissy, my darling little wifey, think well before you break the heart of your Cousin, Eddy." **(3)**

He sealed the letter but held onto it for a moment, agonizing before deciding to reopen it.

Inside it, he placed $5 and added, "I open this letter to enclose the 5$ — I have just received another letter from you announcing the rect. of mine. My heart bleeds for you. Dearest Aunty consider my happiness while you are thinking about your own. I am saving all I can. The only money I have yet spent is 50 cts for washing — I have 2.25 left. I will shortly send you more. Write immediately. I shall be all anxiety & dread until I hear from you. Try and convince my dear Virga. how devotedly I love her. I wish you would get me the Republican which noticed the Messenger & send it on immediately by mail. God bless & protect you both." **(3)**

He walked to the post office, letter in hand, hoping that his fervent plea and his demonstration of responsibility would sway Muddy's decision… and Virginia's. On the

way back, he stopped again at the bar to numb away the

intolerable, aching hole he felt in his very core at the

potential loss of the cousin who he had come to love with

all his soul.

The agony of awaiting Muddy's reply was not something Edgar could face sober. After several days without shaving, bathing or getting a thing done at work, Edgar was called into T.W.'s office. He knew this would be bad but was past caring or thinking about anything other than Virginia.

T.W. eyed him angrily. "You haven't written a goddamned word all week," he said, reproachfully.

"I know." Edgar mumbled, staring at the floor. He had no excuses and didn't care to offer any.

"Every day this week, you have come in reeking of alcohol!" accused T.W. "What has driven you to drink like this?"

Edgar sighed. "The woman I love… has been torn away from me."

T.W. rolled his eyes. At the same instant, however, he remembered what it was like at Edgar's age and was struck with a moment of sympathy.

"Look at me," said T.W.

Edgar forced himself to look up and face him.

"You get the hell out of here and do not come back until you're the confident, energetic young man I hired last month," T.W. said sternly.

Edgar confusedly eyed T.W., not fully grasping what he was saying, before T.W. continued.

"Go get her back."

Edgar nodded his comprehension. He stood up and the two men shook hands, as gentlemen and as friends.

Edgar, clean-shaven and bathed, sat before Muddy at the kitchen table. She regarded him sternly, mulling over what he'd said, as he beseeched her with his eyes. Meanwhile, Virginia watched from several paces away, inside her bedroom with the door cracked open. She silently shook with sobs as she secretly listened.

"You want to marry her," scoffed Muddy, incredulous. "She is thirteen years old, Edgar."

"I know. But I love her. I passionately, devotedly love her," he replied. "I cannot live without her."

Muddy thought, looking at the floor. She did not like this. She looked into his eyes, however, and saw that he was honest. She mused a few moments longer before coming to a decision.

"Alright. But you don't so much as *touch* her until she turns sixteen," Muddy consented, looking him dead in the eye.

Edgar nearly leapt for joy. "Yes, of course!" he agreed.

"Fine," nodded Muddy. "But I will be watching you, and I'll know if you've done anything, and I will kill you with my bare hands."

"Not to worry, Muddy," laughed Edgar. "Nothing more than a peck on the cheek till she's sixteen."

At the crack of her door, Virginia beamed, wiping her tears away.

Virginia looked radiant in the wedding dress that she and Muddy hand-sewed together, the perfect bride despite her young age. Edgar, his hair combed perfectly, sideburns trimmed expertly, wore his rented suit with the air of a perfect gentleman. His grey eyes sparkled as he admired his love, his beautiful cousin who was about to become his wife.

As the ceremony began, they found that they couldn't look at each other lest they burst out laughing at the ancient minister's thick Irish accent. When after what seemed like an eternity he finally announced that Edgar may kiss his bride, Edgar gently, sweetly, with trembling hands, lifted the veil off of Virginia's face. Remembering his promise to

Muddy, he paused, shooting Muddy a terrified look.

Muddy gave him a stern look in the eye, before laughing

and nodding her consent. Edgar kissed Virginia softly,

chastely on the lips, before shocking all the witnesses by

hugging her tightly, lifting her off the ground. T.W. and his

family, Muddy, and even the centenarian minister couldn't

help but laugh. He held her, his eyes shut, a blissful smile

on his face. All was right with the world.

> "I dwelt alone
>
> In a world of moan,
>
> And my soul was a stagnant tide
>
> Till the fair and gentle Eulalie became my
> blushing bride —
>
> Till the yellow-haired young Eulalie became my
> smiling bride." **(4)**

Back at the editor's desk of the *Southern Literary Messenger*, Edgar read and wrote industriously day in, day out, expertly handling all the business of running the magazine. His erudition, commanding tone, detailed analyses and delicious sarcasm forced the literary world to take notice of this fresh new voice, this young gun. With delight and gusto, he wrote his no-holds-barred review of a book that had been promoted relentlessly in the magazines for months as if it were the Second Coming; a book that had been marketed to death in the *New York Mirror* and other widely-read papers using blitzkrieg tactics that Edgar saw right through and thoroughly resented.

"WELL! — here we have it! This is *the* book — *the* book *par excellence* — the book bepuffed, beplastered, and be-*Mirrored*: the book "attributed to" Mr. Blank, and "said to be from the pen" of Mr. Asterisk: the book which has been "about to appear" — "in press" — "in progress" — "in preparation" — and "forthcoming:" the book "graphic" in anticipation — "talented" *a priori* — and God knows what *in prospectu*. For the sake of every thing puffed, puffing, and puffable, let us take a peep at its contents!" Edgar smiled contemptuously, writing his review of *Norman Leslie* by Theodore S. Fay. **(5)**

With his rapier-like pen, he slashed and body-slammed, pulling no punches, exposing the editorial corruption of which this book's inundatory marketing was but one example.

"Norman Leslie, gentle reader, a Tale of the Present Times, is, after all, written by nobody in the world but Theodore S. Fay, and Theodore S. Fay is nobody in the world but "one of the Editors of the *New York Mirror*," he continued. **(5)**

Finished exposing the book's hollow and corrupt marketing, he went on to expose the fact that the book itself was awful… the reading public had been fed a load of bull, and Edgar wasn't about to let this stand.

"As regards Mr. Fay's *style*, it is unworthy of a school-boy. The "Editor of the New York Mirror" has either never seen an edition of Murray's Grammar, or he has been a-Willising so long as to have forgotten his vernacular language. Let us examine one or two of his sentences at random. Page 28, vol. i. "He was doomed to wander through the *fartherest* climes alone and branded." Why not say at once *fartherertherest?* Page 150, vol. i. "Yon kindling orb should be hers; and that faint spark close to its side should teach her how dim and yet how near my soul was to her own." What is the meaning of all this? Is Mr. Leslie's soul dim to her own, as well as near to her own? — for the sentence implies as much. Suppose we say "should teach her how dim was my soul, and yet how near to her own." Page 101, vol. i. "You are both right and both wrong — you, Miss Romain, to judge so harshly of all men who are not versed in the easy elegance of the drawing room, and your father in too great lenity towards men of sense, &c." This is really something new, but we are sorry to say, something incomprehensible. Suppose we translate it. "You are both right and both wrong — you, Miss Romain, are both right and *wrong* to judge so harshly of all not versed in the elegance of the drawing-room, &c.; and your father *is both right and wrong* in too great lenity towards men of sense." —

Mr. Fay, have you ever visited Ireland in your

peregrinations? But the book is full to the brim of

such absurdities, and it is useless to pursue the

matter any farther. There is not a single page of

Norman Leslie in which even a school-boy would fail

to detect at least two or three gross errors in

Grammar, and some two or three most egregious

sins against common-sense." **(5)**

Triumphant, he stood up, corked his ink, massaged a

cramp out of his writing hand, and headed to the printer,

manuscript in hand.

Virginia, Edgar's biggest fan, laughed uncontrollably, tears rolling down her cheeks as she read his *Norman Leslie* review. She was so proud of her brilliant, erudite husband, his wit and his total mastery of his craft. She admired his honesty and courage in standing up for what was right and exposing what was wrong.

They rented a lovely little house on Richmond's Church Hill, which Muddy kept sparkling. They had not a care in the world, as Muddy cooked every meal and did the family's laundry, truly assuming the role of mother for both of them. Edgar's bout of drinking and depression was long behind him. These were productive, creative and happy days until one day T.W. ominously called Edgar into his office once again.

"What's going on?" asked Edgar.

T.W. leaned back in his chair and laced his fingers over his now even larger belly, enriched by the magazine's wild success. T.W. had made a tough judgment call. He knew that Edgar's popular, respected but inflammatory reviews and excellent taste in choosing material to fill the *Messenger's* pages were what had expanded his bank account (and his belly). But Edgar's reviews were increasingly infuriating powerful people and T.W. was getting tired of all the grief that he was getting because of them. It frightened him to have so many people in high places angry at his magazine… these were people that, if enraged enough, could ruin him.

"I'm concerned about all the angry letters we're receiving and what the other magazines are saying about your reviews," said T.W.

"About my reviews?" scoffed Edgar.

"They're saying that they're too harsh," explained T.W.

"They're truthful. I'm just saying what needs to be said but that no one else has the fortitude to say," replied Edgar.

"I'm not sure that's the position I want my magazine in," said T.W. "I don't want to participate in an all-out war, and that's where you're leading us."

"So… what are you saying?" asked Edgar, becoming nervous.

T.W. slid a check across his desk to Edgar. Edgar, confused and taken aback, flinched and eyed T.W. inquisitively.

"You're fired, Edgar," said T.W. "This is two weeks' severance. That ought to keep you out of trouble while you look for a new journal to edit."

This was hard for T.W. He had come to genuinely like this young man, but he had to look out for his own interests. He coldly sat back, replacing his hands over his belly.

Edgar stared at him, speechless, incredulous.

The Poe family moved to New York. "It's the center of the literary world," Edgar explained to a skeptical Muddy and Virginia. They had really liked living in Richmond, but there were no other opportunities there, and despite their misgivings, they trusted and stood by their Edgar. They rented a tiny apartment, barely big enough for one person, never mind a family of three. Muddy scrimped and saved, stretching every dollar. Edgar wrote all night and spent all day visiting the magazines to look for work and to sell his tales, poems and articles. He was also trying out a new genre, the novel, working on his *The Narrative of Arthur Gordon Pym of Nantucket.* Virginia, blossoming into a knockout beauty that elicited stares from men and envious glances from women at the literary salons that the couple attended, did everything she could to support and encourage her man. She cleaned and arranged his pens, keeping them in good working order. She organized his papers and dusted his books. She wished there were more that she could do. Her sixteenth birthday was approaching, and she knew that meant that there soon would be.

Muddy was out shopping for groceries while Edgar industriously wrote at the apartment's tiny writing desk. Virginia dusted and tidied, watching her husband all the while. He was too lost in thought to notice that he was being watched. She thought, biting her lip, before coming to a decision. She softly walked behind him, leaned over to whisper in his ear and gently stroked the back of his neck.

"You know… we're alone. Mother won't be back for hours," she said.

Edgar shut his eyes, put his pen down and took a deep breath.

"I promised your mother not till you're sixteen. Please don't make this any more difficult than it is. I think if you continue to breathe on me, I'll explode," he stammered.

Virginia continued to stroke the back of his neck, leaned in even more closely and whispered, "I turn sixteen in two weeks. Close enough."

She didn't have to tell him twice. He stood up, spun around and scooped her up in his arms. They kissed passionately as he carried her down the hall and deftly kicked the door shut behind them.

Lying together on one of their bedroom's two beds, still sweaty, flushed and blissful, Edgar and Virginia talked, their fingers interlaced, her head resting on his chest.

"As much as I don't want to, we should get dressed before she gets back," breathed Edgar.

"Yes," giggled Virginia, "I don't want you to get in trouble. At least we only have to pretend to be celibate for two weeks."

Edgar laughed then abruptly stopped, terrified.

"I think I hear someone on the stairs," he said.

They sprang up, threw on their clothes as fast as they could, straightened their hair as best as possible and dashed out into the living room.

Edgar dove into his writing chair, his shirt misbuttoned but otherwise looking as if nothing had happened. Virginia smoothed her dress and grabbed her feather duster, trying to appear the same. The door opened and Muddy, as pale as if she'd seen a ghost, sadly entered.

Edgar and Virginia shared a terrified look, wondering for a split second if she could somehow know…

"The bank… all the banks… have collapsed," she said, her voice shaking.

"What?!" demanded Virginia, shocked.

"All the banks are shut down," explained Muddy. "Thank God we have the cash that we have, and that we didn't get it earlier, when I might have deposited it…"

The three of them scanned each other's faces for ideas and answers as to what to do now.

The answer was Philadelphia. A new literary magazine had just been launched there. Edgar wrote to the proprietor and offered his services. The proprietor, William Burton, an actor whose megalomaniacal leanings caused him to believe that his presence and opinions were needed in the world of literature as well as the theater, was aware of Edgar through having read his work and his reviews in the *Southern Literary Messenger*. He was impressed by the numbers he'd heard; Edgar's firebrand reviews and titillating horror tales had driven the *SLM*'s subscriptions through the roof, more than doubling the magazine's subscribers during his short tenure. Seeing dollar signs and worldwide fame, Burton hired Edgar as editor.

The family had high hopes for this situation, but Burton was unfortunately even more illiterate and far less of a businessman than T.W. White. Burton didn't have the faintest idea of what was involved in running a magazine and quickly lost interest. It became a side-project for him, secondary by a wide margin to his theater career. When he toured with his theater company (which was most of the time), responsibility for the magazine's entire operations fell to Edgar, all for the pittance of $10 per week. Edgar was strapped for time and for money. He had hardly any time for his own writing after he finished reading and reviewing tome after tome of inanity, choosing corny woodcuts to accompany nauseating sentimental poems, dropping the whole mess off at the printer and proofreading. In the time that remained, to make ends meet, he solicited and solved cryptograms in *Alexander's Weekly Messenger.*

By candlelight, Edgar stayed up night after night solving readers' cryptographic creations. Most were child's play for him. Occasionally, someone with half a brain would send one in and he'd actually have to work at it. Tonight, he was working on one that was pretty good. He was fully absorbed in it and genuinely enjoying it, but he was so, so tired after many chaotic days and many nights of burning the midnight oil. For the moment, he was stumped. He ran his hands through his messy curls, which were at this point going in every direction. He rubbed his eyes. He swore. He laid his head down on the table, "just for a second."

Virginia stretched and yawned as she strolled into the kitchen. She jumped, startled, as she came upon Edgar, still asleep at the kitchen table, with the brilliant light of sunrise streaming over him. She gasped, horrified that her Eddy had spent his night like this. She quietly approached and laid her hand on his shoulder.

"Darling," she said, softly.

He didn't budge.

"Eddy!" she whispered, gently shaking his shoulder.

"Huh?!" he grunted, startled awake. He groggily sat up and frowned in confusion as Virginia began to laugh.

"Eddy, you're wearing your work," she explained. He'd slept with his face pressed to the paper all night, and his cheek was covered in all manner of arcane symbols. "How late were you up last night?"

"I don't even know," he replied, rubbing his face.

Virginia grabbed a towel and wet it in a nearby basin. "Here, let me clean you up," she said, dabbing at his face. "It's almost time for you to go to work."

"Shit," he swore.

"I'm worried about you, working this much," she said, laying the towel down and sitting on his lap. She kissed him.

"What's this you were working on last night, this… gobbledygook?" she asked.

He sighed. "Burton's doesn't pay enough to make ends meet. To make up the rest, I'm soliciting cryptograms from readers of Alexander's Weekly Messenger. It's been successful… *too* successful. The readers are really having fun with it and cryptograms are pouring in as fast as I can write the solutions."

"This one has really thrown me," he continued, gesturing to the one that had given him such trouble the night before. "I don't know if I'll be able to solve it."

"Of course you will," said Virginia, sweetly kissing him again. "But not if you don't get any sleep. Promise me you'll come to bed at a sane hour tonight."

Edgar smiled at his lovely, devoted bride and nodded.

On a sunny Saturday, Edgar decided to heed his wife's advice and take a break. He brought her along; he had found a wonderful place that he wanted to show her.

Holding hands, talking and laughing, they walked along a trail, then off the trail, till they reached the stunningly beautiful Wissahiccon. Sunlight shone in between the trees and glinted off of the clear, tranquilly moving water. The gorge was lush and green; the Wissahiccon cut through steep, rocky cliffs. Virginia gasped at its beauty. Edgar smiled, held out his hand and beckoned her down to the water. He climbed masterfully, assisting her all the way. When they reached the bottom, they were hot and sweaty. Edgar took off his shirt, rolled up his pants and jumped into the deliciously cool water. He held his arms out toward

Virginia, encouraging her to join him. She was skeptical at

first, but both the water and her husband looked so inviting,

she stripped down to her muslin underdress and gingerly

stepped in. She laughed and winced at the shocking cold of

the water in contrast with the hot, humid summer air.

Taking her hand, Edgar floated on his back. Virginia took

his cue and did the same. They floated, letting the gentle

current carry them until they arrived at what Edgar wanted

her to see. He pointed to it and she turned to see a

preternaturally beautiful meadow. She turned to him and

smiled broadly, honored that he wanted to share this

wonder with her.

Under a huge, old angel oak, Edgar and Virginia chatted and laughed, their hair still wet, as they enjoyed a lunch of apples and a rabbit that Edgar had hunted, roasting it over a campfire. The bright sunlight and the clear blue sky accentuated the green of the grass and the colors of the wildflowers. "Magic," Virginia thought.

"I've been working on some conundrums for Alexander's," Edgar said. "Want to hear them?"

"Of course!" said Virginia, beginning to laugh in anticipation.

"Why is a tin cup like a crab?" Edgar began.

"I don't know," Virginia dutifully replied.

"Because it is a can, sir." **(6)**

Virginia cracked up. "Oh, that's horrible!" she exclaimed. Edgar grinned from ear to ear. He loved making his wife laugh and no one loved his puns more than she did.

"When you called the dock a wharf, why was it a deed of writing?" he asked.

"Do tell," replied Virginia.

"Because it was a dock you meant," he delivered. **(6)**

Virginia laughed and laughed, doubled over. This one really got her.

Delighted, laughing himself at his wife's hysterical laughter, Edgar continued.

"Alright, one more… Why ought the author of 'The Grotesque and Arabesque' to be a good writer of verses?"

Virginia paused, pondering this for a moment before shaking her head and looking at him expectantly.

"Because he's a *poet* to *a t*." **(6)**

After pausing for a second to muse, she got the punchline and her laughter echoed throughout the meadow.

Exhausted and mildly sunburned but deliriously happy, the Poes walked home hand in hand as the sun set. As they reached their home, Edgar stopped Virginia.

"What?" she asked.

"Close your eyes," Edgar said.

"What? Why?" Virginia giggled, wondering what he was up to.

"Just trust me," he said softly.

"Alright," she laughed. "You haven't steered me wrong yet."

Edgar guided her gently onto the porch and through the front door, holding her hand.

"OK. You can open your eyes now," he said.

When she saw the piano that had appeared in the living room, she nearly fainted. She grabbed tightly onto Edgar's arm to keep from falling over. Tears sprang to her eyes and she turned to him, agape.

"Eddy…" she stammered. "It's amazing. I love it!"

She kissed him before he could reply.

"But Eddy… we can't afford this," she said, frowning.

"We can afford anything you need, " Edgar gallantly replied. "I've arranged for a piano teacher to come three times a week to teach you how to play."

A tear rolled down Virginia's cheek. She beamed pure gratitude at him, speechless.

Virginia sewed while Muddy cooked the family

breakfast as Edgar read the morning paper. Suddenly, he

slapped the newspaper onto the kitchen table and yelled,

"That son of a bitch!"

Virginia, startled, asked, "My God, what??"

"Burton." Edgar replied, through gritted teeth. "That

imbecilic tub of lard is selling the *Gentleman's Magazine*."

"What? And this is the first you've heard of this?"

asked Muddy, alarmed.

"Yes, why bother telling the magazine's editor? He

doesn't need to know a silly little thing like that," swore

Edgar. "Why would a man need to know that the magazine

he edits for a pittance that barely allows his family to squeak by is being sold out from under him?"

Virginia set her sewing down and covered her eyes. Edgar breathed a big sigh. He didn't want her or Muddy to worry.

"Fear not, darling," he said calmly, taking Virginia's hand. "If I've learned anything from working for two unlettered hinds like White and Burton, it's that to be controlled is to be ruined. To have to coin one's brain into silver, at the nod of a master, is the hardest thing in the world." **(7) (8)**

Virginia looked up at him.

"I'm sick to death of working my fingers to the bone only for us barely to survive while magazine owners get fat off of my labors," he said.

"I'm going to launch my own magazine."

Virginia smiled and squeezed his hand.

"I've always thought you'd do best as your own boss," she replied, wrapping her arms around his neck and kissing him.

PROSPECTUS OF THE PENN MAGAZINE, A MONTHLY LITERARY JOURNAL, TO BE EDITED AND PUBLISHED IN THE CITY OF PHILADELPHIA, BY EDGAR A. POE. — *To the Public.* — Since resigning the conduct of The Southern Literary Messenger, at the commencement of its third year, I have constantly held in view the establishment of a Magazine which should retain some of the chief features of that Journal, abandoning the rest. Delay, however, has been occasioned by a variety of causes, and not until now have I felt fully prepared to execute the intention.

I will be pardoned for speaking more directly of The Messenger. Having in it no proprietary right, my objects too, in many respects, being at variance with those of its very worthy owner, I found difficulty in stamping upon its pages that *individuality* which I believe essential to the perfect success of all similar publications. In regard to their permanent interest and influence, it has appeared to me that a continuous and definite character, with a marked certainty of purpose, was of the most vital importance; and these desiderata, it is obvious, can never be surely attained where more than one mind has the general direction of the undertaking. This consideration has been an inducement to found a Magazine of my own, as the only chance of carrying out to full completion whatever peculiar designs I may have entertained.

To those who remember the early years of The Messenger, it will be scarcely necessary to say that its main feature was somewhat overdone causticity in its department of Critical Notices. The Penn Magazine will retain this trait of severity in so much only as the calmest and sternest sense of literary justice will permit. One or two years, since elapsed, may have mellowed down the petulance, without interfering with the rigor of the critic. Most surely they have not yet taught him to read through the medium of a publisher's interest, nor convinced him of the impolicy of speaking the truth. It shall be the first and chief purpose of the Magazine now proposed, to become known as one where may be found, at all times, and upon all subjects, an honest and a fearless opinion. This is a purpose of which no man need be ashamed. It is one, moreover, whose novelty at least will give it interest. For assurance that I will fulfil it in its best spirit, and to the very letter, I appeal with confidence to the many thousands of my friends, and especially of my Southern friends, who sustained me in The Messenger, where I had but a partial opportunity of completing my own plans.

In respect to the other general features of the Penn Magazine, a few words here will suffice. Upon matters of *very* grave moment, it will leave the task of instruction in better hands. Its aim, chiefly, shall be to *please*; and this through means of versatility, originality and pungency. It must not be supposed, however, that the intention is never to be serious. There *is* a species of grave writing, of which the spirit

is novelty and vigor, and the immediate object of the
enkindling of the imagination. In such productions,
belonging to the loftiest regions of literature, the
journal shall abound. It may be as well here to
observe, that nothing said in this Prospectus should
he construed into a design of sullying the Magazine
with any tincture of the buffoonery, scurrility, or
profanity, which are the blemish of some of the most
vigorous of the European prints. In all branches of
the literary department, the best aid, from the
highest and purest sources, is secured.

To the mechanical execution of the work the
greatest attention will be given which such a matter
can require. In this respect, it is proposed to
surpass, by very much, the ordinary Magazine style.
The form will nearly resemble that of The
Knickerbocker. The paper will be equal to that of The
North American Review. The pictorial
embellishments will be numerous, and by the leading
artists of the country, but will be only introduced in
the necessary illustration of the text.

The Penn Magazine will be published in
Philadelphia, on the first of each month, and will
form, half yearly, a volume of about 500 pages. The
price will be $5 per annum, payable in advance, or
upon the receipt of the first number, which will be
issued on the first of January, 1841. **(9)**

Virginia stood before her piano, hands clasped, nervously excited to sing and play for Edgar and Muddy for the first time. An accomplished singer and pianist with a natural talent for both, she was confident that she'd thoroughly impress them. Edgar loved her voice and Muddy bragged to anyone who would listen about her daughter's skill as a pianist.

Virginia smiled at Edgar and Muddy and sat down before her piano.

"Alright," she grinned. "Here it is."

"Tell me the tales that to me were so dear,

Long, long ago, long, long ago,

Sing me the songs I delighted to hear,

Long, long ago, long ago,

Now you are come all my grief is removed,

Let me forget that so long you have roved.

Let me believe that you love as you loved,

Long, long ago, long ago." (**10**)

Muddy tightly clutched a handkerchief, fighting back tears, her daughter's singing was so beautiful. Edgar was rapt, agape at his wife's beauty and talent. Virginia continued,

"Do you remember the paths where we met?

Long, long ago, long, long ago.

Ah, yes, you told me you'd never forget," (**10**)

Virginia's voice cracked. She rolled her eyes, mildly embarrassed, but sang on.

"Long, long ago, long ago.

Then to all others, my smile you preferred," **(10)**

She coughed. She tried to recover and continue, but was gripped by a coughing fit. Edgar and Muddy's smiles became looks of concern. Her coughing grew more and more violent until suddenly, blood shot out of her mouth and pale, she collapsed to the floor.

Edgar leapt out of his chair and dove to Virginia. His eyes wide, his hands shaking, his heart pounding, he wrapped his arms around her and lifted her up to sitting. She tightly gripped his arms, staring intently into his eyes, struggling to breathe.

"Sissy?? Sissy??!" he yelled, terrified, as her blood soaked his shirt.

Muddy stood speechless, panicking.

Edgar screamed, "GO GET THE DOCTOR!!"

Wordlessly, Muddy nodded and ran out the front door, leaving it hanging open.

Edgar, his shirt covered in dried blood, sat beside the bed, holding Virginia's hand. Winter dawn threw pink and purple light onto the walls. Haggard and terrified, Edgar closely watched his wife's chest weakly rise and fall, shuddering with every struggling breath. Propped up on pillows, she slept, deathly pale, her cheeks reddened, her forehead beaded with sweat.

Muddy stood in the doorway with the doctor, whispering.

"All you can do is keep her comfortable, keep her propped up like this to keep her airway as clear as possible," whispered the doctor.

"Yes, doctor," replied Muddy, her face streaked by a night of sobbing. "Is there anything we can give her, any medicine?"

"Yes," nodded the doctor. "Jew's Beer, which acts as an expectorant. It can be gotten at any pharmacy."

Muddy nodded. Her face knotted into a sob. "Is there any hope of her making a full recovery?" she asked, her voice breaking.

"I'm afraid not," answered the doctor clinically. "Tuberculosis is very unpredictable, however. She could hang on for years, or she may not make it through today."

Edgar flew out of his chair, knocking it over, and got in the doctor's face, his grey eyes flashing.

"You had better hope she didn't hear that. There will be *no* talk of such things. She *will* recover fully, we'll do whatever we have to, to ensure it!" he yelled.

Muddy gently pulled Edgar away, looking apologetically at the shaken doctor, and guided him back to his seat at Virginia's bedside. She picked the chair back up and he docilely sat back down, resuming his vigil.

Virginia lied propped up on pillows on the couch, drinking Jew's Beer and wincing at the taste, her every breath rattling and audible. She was pale and weak, but at least improved enough to come out to the living room for a few hours a day to enjoy Edgar's company and the sunlight from the front window.

There was a knock at the front door. Virginia was too weak to get up, so Edgar came running in from the kitchen to get it.

"Thomas!" Edgar said, grinning. "Thank you for coming."

Edgar's dear friend Frederick Thomas stepped in, looking around and doing his best to conceal his shock at the family's obvious poverty.

"Of course," replied Thomas, as the two gentlemen shook hands. "I wouldn't miss an opportunity to see my old friend Poe. Not to mention to meet your lovely wife!"

Virginia was embarrassed that she was sick and couldn't get up, but she nodded gracefully and breathed a greeting.

Thomas was taken aback by her classic beauty, which was highlighted by the pallor and rosy cheeks of tuberculosis. "Edgar is a lucky man," he thought, before catching himself staring a little too long.

"Please, make yourself at home. Would you like some tea?" Edgar asked his guest. "And Sissy, would you?"

Thomas and Virginia each happily accepted a cup of freshly brewed, steaming tea.

The tea felt good on Virginia's raw throat, as she listened to the men get reacquainted, laughing about old exploits and planning new.

"So what took a literary man like you to Washington?" asked Edgar.

"I've obtained a clerkship," replied Thomas. "I stroll into the office about nine A.M., and go home around two. This schedule alone allows me plenty of leisure time in which to write, and even during my few hours in the office, it's so easy and my desk has everything I need for writing in apple-pie order, I spend most of my time there writing, too." **(11)**

Edgar and Virginia shared a conspiratory look.

Edgar cleared his throat. "If you don't mind… and please forgive me if I'm being nosy… how much could one make from a job such as this?"

"Fifteen hundred a year," replied Thomas, sipping his tea and grinning. "Would you like me to look into getting you a similar situation?"

Edgar was flabbergasted. "My God, yes. Please do! It would put me out of all difficulty… it would break me out of my current prison of literary drudgery and would end all worry about mere subsistence… That would even be enough for me *finally* to launch my own magazine."

Thomas was delighted. This was why he had come. He and Henry Poe had been close friends in Baltimore before he and Edgar had ever met. They were practically family and Thomas really wanted to help him.

"I happen to be good friends with Robert Tyler, the President's son," said Thomas. "I'll talk to him and see what I can get set in motion for you."

"Please tell him I was a clerk in the Army. I went to West Point! I am perfectly suited for a government job," replied Edgar, excited.

"I happen to know," said Thomas, "That there will soon be a shakeup at the Philadelphia Custom House and many positions will be opening up."

Edgar practically levitated with hope and excitement. Virginia looked heavenward, permeated by a feeling of absolute relief. Help was on the way.

The Poes eagerly awaited word from Thomas. Edgar scanned the newspaper daily for removals and hirings at the Custom House. He was so confident that he would get a place and so focused on it that during this time he hardly wrote. He didn't bother trying to find another editorship. He didn't try to sell any articles. But the weeks dragged on and became months. The Poes lived on bread and molasses for weeks at a time, all becoming thin and haggard, particularly Edgar, who often gave up his share for Virginia, who needed it more.

Edgar wrote to his friend in desperation.

Philadelphia, August 27, '42.
My Dear Thomas,

How happens it that I have received not a line from you for these four months? What in the world is the matter? I write to see if you are still in the land of the living, or have gone your way to the "land o' the leal." I wrote a few words to you, about two months since, from New York, at the importunate demand of W. Wallace, in which you were requested to use your influence, &c. He overlooked me while I wrote, & therefore I could not speak of private matters. I presume you gave the point as much consideration as it demanded, & no more.

What have you been doing for so long a time? I am anxious to learn how you succeed in Washington. I suppose Congress will have adjourned by the time you get this. Since I heard from you I have had a reiteration of the promise, about the Custom-House appointment, from Rob Tyler. A friend of mine, Mr. Jas. Herron, having heard from me casually, that I had some hope of an appointment, called upon R. T., who assured him that I should *certainly* have it & desired him so to inform me. I have, also, paid my respects to Gen. J. W. Tyson, the leader of the T. party in the city, who seems especially well disposed — but, notwithstanding *all this*, I have my doubts. A few days will end them. If I do not get the office, I am just where I started. Nothing more can be done to secure it than has been already done. Literature is at a sad discount. There is really nothing to be done in this way. Without an international copyright law, American authors may as well cut their throats. A good magazine, of the true stamp, would do wonders in the way of a general revivification of letters, or the law. We must have — both if possible.

What has become of Dow? Do you ever see him?

Write immediately & tell me the Washington news.

My poor little wife still continues ill. I have scarcely a faint hope of her recovery.

Remember us all to your friends & believe me your true friend,

Edgar A Poe **(12)**

Scanning the newspaper one morning, Edgar saw something out of the corner of his eye that nearly made him spit his coffee. At the Custom House, there had been four removals and appointments. One of the appointments was for a Mr. Pogue. He leapt out of his chair, his eyes wild, and ran straight to the Custom House.

There, he confirmed his suspicion that "Pogue" had been a misprint. There was no such person. They must have meant *him!* He went to see the Collector of Customs, Mr. Smith and explained the situation. Smith looked up from his paperwork only briefly, considered Edgar for a moment, then looked right back down. Edgar insisted that he swear him in. Smith, this time not even looking up, replied nonchalantly, "I will *send* for you, Mr. Poe."

Edgar went home and waited. Days passed and in a state of high anxiety, he went to see Smith again.

"I've heard through a friend that Robert Tyler has requested that you appoint me," Edgar demanded.

Smith looked quizzically at Edgar.

"Who??" he asked.

"Robert Tyler," Edgar sighed, exasperated. "The son of the President!"

"I have received *no* orders to make *any* further appointments from *President* Tyler, and shall make none!" growled Smith. "Now get the hell out of my office! If and when I receive orders to appoint you, I will *send* for you!"

Debts owing by the Petitioner:

Names of Creditors	Residence	nature of debt	Amount
J. W. Allbright	Philad. 5th bel. Chest.	Note of hand	119.11
J. P. Cowell	9th & Chesnut Sts.	" " "	7.30
Isaac abell & Linwood	d. & Chesnut Sts	" " "	32.05
Benj. Matthias	Vine Street	" " "	20.00
Chas. Rateau & Son	Chesnut bel. 3d	" " "	115.50
John L. Fredericks	d. above Walnut	Rent due	50.00
Dr. Wm. Klapp	d. above Chesnut	Meds. attendance	abt. 50.00
Dr. Wm. Brinckle	Arch near 13th	do do	50.00
John Gray & Son	d. & Christian	Book debt	40.71
M. Vanderfield &	[illegible]	do	13.[illegible]
J. A. Turner	d. & Sen[illegible]	do	19.50
Jas. E. Caldwell	Chesnut near 3d	do	12.00
Wm. C. Burton	11th & [illegible]	[illegible]	100.00
Nicholas Biddle	Spruce & 7th	money advanced	20.00
Rich. L. Krinkle	[illegible]	Book debt	15.00
Roberts Walter & Cottenham	[illegible]	Book debt	6.00
Ann Hughes	d. bel. Christ.	Sal. of a [illegible]	5.00
Thomas Mills	[illegible]	Rent debt	24.00
Hugh Oles	J. near Vine	do	8.00
Chas. [illegible]	Chesnut bel. 8th	do	4.00
John C. Cox	[illegible]	money loan	30.00
Col. Wm. Drayton	S. Petersburg, Va.	do	100.00
Louis A. Godey	Chesnut above 3d	do	60.00

144

Name	Location	Occupation	Amount
Ezra [illegible]	" "	do	20.00
[Nicol] McCrery	Richmond Va	clerk of court	130.51
Chas. [Palmer]	do	do	135.00
C. G. [Carruthers]	do	Bookseller	129.50
J. W. Franklin	do	do	9.00
Rich [Savage]	do	do [illegible]	10.00
Augustus [illegible]	do	do	25.00
Phillip A. [Taylor]	do	[auctioneer]	40.00
[illegible] Henderson	do	[merchant]	20.00
David [Bridges]	do	"	30.00
R. C. Gall	do	"	75.00
Wm Gall	do	"	90.00
A. S. [Howard]	do	"	150.00
Rob. [Stannard &c]	do	"	11.00
A. N. Reynolds	New Orleans city	"	50.00
Wm Cullen Bryant	do	"	31.00
S. A. [Paulding]	do	[Bookseller]	40.00
N. Parsons	do	[merchant, printer]	50.00
[illegible] Jacobs	do	Bookseller about	30.00
[illegible] Nissan	do	do	15.00
[Anna] Grant	[illegible]	[illegible]	27.50
[illegible] [illegible]	[illegible]	[illegible]	[illegible]

Schedule B—referred to in the annexed Petition.

The property of the Petitioner consists of the following particulars:

The Petitioner is possessed of no Property, real, personal or mixed, beyond his wearing apparel, and a few printed sheets, of no use to any one else, and of no value to any one.

Attest
W. Hopkinson
Commr

[signature]

United States, *Eastern* }
District of *Pennsylvania* }

ON this *19th* day of *November* A. D. 18*40*.
before me the Subscriber, *a commissioner in Bankruptcy*, personally appeared the above named

Edgar A. Poe

who subscribed the foregoing Petition and Schedules in my presence, and *made oath*

that according to the best of *his* knowledge and belief, the facts stated in *his* Petition and Schedules aforesaid, are true as therein stated.

Sworn & Subscribed before me   J Hopkinson   Commissioner   *Edgar A. Poe*

(13)

147

PROSPECTUS

OF

THE STYLUS:

A Monthly Journal of General Literature

TO BE EDITED BY

EDGAR A. POE

And published, in the city of Philadelphia, by

CLARKE & POE.

----- unbending that all men
Of thy firm TRUTH may say – "Lo! this is writ
With the antique *iron pen*."

Launcelot Canning

To the Public. — The Prospectus of a Monthly
Journal to have been called "THE PENN MAGAZINE,"
has already been partially circulated.
Circumstances, in which the public have no interest,
induced a suspension of the project, which is now,
under the best auspices, resumed, with no other
modification than that of the title. "The Penn
Magazine," it has been thought, was a name
somewhat too local in its suggestions, and "THE
STYLUS" has been finally adopted.

It has become obvious, indeed, to even the most
unthinking, that the period has at length arrived
when a journal of the character here proposed, is
demanded and will be sustained. The late
movements on the great question of International
Copy-Right, are but an index of the universal *disgust*
excited by what is quaintly termed the *cheap*
literature of the day: — as if that which is uttcrly
worthless in itself, can be cheap at any price under
the sun.

"The Stylus" will include about one hundred royal
octavo pages, in single column, per month; forming
two thick volumes per year. In its mechanical
appearance — in its typography, paper and binding
— it will far surpass all American journals of its
kind. Engravings, when used, will be in the highest
style of Art, but are promised only in obvious
illustration of the text, and in strict keeping with the
Magazine character. Upon application to the
proprietors, by any agent of repute who may desire
the work, or by any other individual who may feel

interested, a specimen sheet will be forwarded. As, for many reasons, it is inexpedient to commence a journal of this kind at any other period than at the beginning or middle of the year, the first number of "The Stylus" will not be regularly issued until the first of July, 1843. In the meantime, to insure its perfect and permanent success, no means will be left untried which long experience, untiring energy, and the amplest capital, can supply. The price will be *Five Dollars* per annum, or *Three Dollars* per single volume, in advance. Letters which concern only the Editorial management may be addressed to Edgar A. Poe, individually; all others to Clarke & Poe.

The necessity for any very rigid definition of the literary character or aims of "The Stylus," is, in some measure, obviated by the general knowledge, on the part of the public, of the editor's connexion, formerly, with the two most successful periodicals in the country — "The Southern Literary Messenger," and "Graham's Magazine." Having no proprietary right, however, in either of these journals; his objects, too, being, in many respects, at variance with those of their very worthy owners; he found it not only impossible to effect anything, on the score of taste, for the mechanical appearance of the works, but exceedingly difficult, also, to stamp, upon their internal character, that *individuality* which he believes essential to the full success of all similar publications. In regard to their extensive and permanent influence, it appears to him that continuity, definitiveness, and a marked certainty of purpose, are requisites of vital importance; and he cannot help thinking that these requisites are attainable, only where a single mind has at least *the general* direction of the enterprise. Experience, in a word, has distinctly shown him — what, indeed, might have been demonstrated *à priori* — that in founding a Magazine wherein his interest should be not merely editorial, lies his sole chance of carrying out to completion whatever peculiar intentions he may have entertained.

In many important points, then, the new journal will differ widely from either of those named. It will endeavor to be at the same time more varied and more *unique*; — more vigorous, more pungent, more original, more individual, and more independent. It will discuss not only the Belles-Lettres, but, very thoroughly, the Fine Arts, with the Drama: and, more in brief, will give, each month, a Retrospect of our Political History. It will enlist the loftiest talent, but employ it not always in the loftiest — at least not always in the most pompous or Puritanical way. It will aim at affording a fair and not dishonorable field for the *true* intellect of the land, without reference to the mere *prestige* of celebrated names. It will support the general interests of the Republic of Letters, and insist upon regarding the world at large as the sole proper audience for the author. It will resist the dictation of Foreign Reviews. It will eschew the stilted dulness of our own Quarterlies, and while it *may*, if necessary, be no less learned, will deem it wiser to be less anonymous, and difficult to be more dishonest, than they.

An important feature of the work, and one which will be introduced in the opening number, will be a series of *Critical* and *Biographical Sketches* of *American Writers*. These Sketches will be accompanied with full length and characteristic portraits; will include every person of literary note in America; and will investigate carefully and with rigorous impartiality, the individual claims of each.

It shall, in fact, be the *chief purpose* of "The Stylus," to become known as a journal wherein may be found, at all times, upon all subjects within its legitimate reach, a sincere and a fearless opinion. It shall be a leading object to assert in precept, and to maintain in practice, the rights, while, in effect, it demonstrates the advantages, of an absolutely independent criticism; — a criticism self-sustained; guiding itself only by the purest rules of Art; analyzing and urging these rules as it applies them; holding itself aloof from all personal bias; and acknowledging no fear save that of outraging the Right.

CLARKE & POE.

N. B. Those friends of the Proprietors, throughout the country, who may feel disposed to support "The Stylus," will confer an important favor by sending in their names *at once*.

The provision in respect to payment '*in advance*', is intended only as a general rule, and has reference to the Magazine *when established*. In the commencement, the subscription money will not be demanded until the issue of the second number.

C. & P. **(14)**

At long last, Smith's unprofessional gruffness got him fired. The second Edgar read of this in the paper, he packed his bags for a trip to Washington, D.C., taking matters into his own hands. He'd secure a meeting with the President and ask him for a clerkship *himself.*

Before leaving, he hugged Muddy and kissed Virginia. Both were proud of him, impressed with his drive and filled with hope at the idea of Edgar having a steady job that would provide for their present and allow him to build his magazine for the future.

Edgar walked through the D.C. streets, nervously checking the scrap of paper on which he'd written Thomas' address. Finally, he found it: Fuller's Hotel.

He went upstairs, a spring in his step, and knocked on the door.

As the door opened, Edgar could see and hear Thomas miserably hacking and coughing, sheet-white and feverish in bed.

"Dow?" he asked quizzically, as Jesse Dow, the men's mutual friend, opened the door and slinked out, quietly shutting it behind him.

"I'm afraid Thomas is very ill," said Dow. "He came down with a fever, chills and a dreadful cough and has been confined to bed for several days. He's asked me to accompany you to tonight's festivities in his stead."

"Who will accompany me to see the President tomorrow?" asked Edgar, becoming nervous.

"Robert Tyler has agreed to," replied Dow. "I'll introduce you to him formally tonight."

Edgar nodded and anxiously ran his hand through his hair.

"Mr. Tyler and I will meet you downstairs after you get settled in," said Dow, giving Edgar an encouraging pat on the shoulder. Edgar forced half a smile.

In the hotel bar, Dow led Edgar to a table where a young, handsome, brooding man sat drinking. The man stood up and smiled broadly when he saw them approach.

"You must be the fabled Poe!" he grinned, shaking Edgar's hand. "Robert Tyler."

The three men exchanged pleasantries and sat down.

"If you come to my room at ten o'clock tomorrow morning," said Robert, "I'll be happy to take you to see my father."

"Thank you very much for your time and your assistance," replied Edgar, trying his best to sound cordial while fighting a monstrous case of nerves. He chewed his lip, his grey eyes flashing as they darted quickly around the room.

"I don't know about you gentlemen," said Robert, leaning back in his chair, "But I could use a drink."

"I'm with you," replied Dow. "I hear Fuller's Port is excellent."

Edgar hesitated, knowing his tendencies with alcohol, before relenting and deciding to calm his nerves.

Robert confidently, cavalierly ordered three glasses of Port from a passing waiter. Edgar sipped his slowly, beginning to perspire as he drank. He took off his cloak and draped it over the back of his chair. He loosened his cravat. Dow and Robert talked and laughed, but Edgar could only occasionally muster a forced smile. Finally, hoping to medicate his anxiety away, he downed the last of his Port in one gulp.

"Another for you, Poe?" asked Robert, the consummate host.

"Why not?" he breathed, the alcohol taking effect.

Dow ordered another round. As Edgar began drinking his second Port, Robert stood up and gestured someone over to the table. Thomas Dunn English, a man with a ridiculous, over-the-top moustache, dressed in too-tight, foppish clothes, strutted over and joined the men at the table.

Edgar glanced at him sidelong, wondering who this silly-looking creature was and whether he thought he was impressing anyone with his obviously *tres recherché* look.

"Now, correct me if you gentlemen have already met in literary circles in Philadelphia, but if you haven't, English, this is Edgar Allan Poe," Robert introduced them.

"Pleasure to make your acquaintance," replied English, nodding to Poe. "You write for Graham's, don't you?"

"I wrote for Graham's, yes," replied Edgar. "I've since struck out on my own to create a magazine that's worth reading, where fine literature isn't dragged down by cloying love-doggerel and fashion plates featuring mustachioed imbeciles in effeminately-cut suits."

Oops.

Dow and Robert's eyes widened. Edgar blushed as he realized how this might be taken by the present company and quickly downed the rest of his Port. He was angry at himself. Had he not had two drinks in him, his tongue wouldn't have been loosened and he wouldn't have let his contempt for this obvious wanker fly. He loosened his collar and flopped back in his chair.

"What brings you to D.C., Mr. Poe?" asked English, attempting to end an uncomfortable pause.

"I'm here to secure a clerkship at the Philadelphia Custom House," Edgar confidently replied.

"Really!" English smiled a smile that dripped with evil. "My father is Inspector of Customs there. I'll be sure to put in a good word for you."

With that, English finished his drink and stalked away.

Dow and Robert shared a look of disbelief at how poorly that went.

"Let's get you some coffee," Dow said to Edgar.

"Capital idea," he slurred.

"I'm going to turn in," said Robert, wanting no part of the rest of this evening that had gone off the rails. "See you tomorrow, Poe."

Carrying a mug of coffee through thick cigar smoke, Dow frantically looked around for Edgar.

"English," he called, "have you seen Poe? I'm trying to get some coffee into him."

"Looks like he's found himself some," English said, gesturing snidely toward the bar.

"Shit!" swore Dow, running to the bar with the coffee. "That's Fuller's famous rum-and-coffee!"

Dow reached Edgar, who was wearing his cloak inside out and could hardly hold his head up.

"Bartender, another!" slurred Edgar.

"That's the last thing you need," said Dow. Dow took him by the hand and tried to drag him away from the bar, but Edgar fell flat on his face, passed out.

Dow and a sweaty, feverish Thomas dragged Edgar down the hallway to his room.

"What the hell happened?" asked Thomas, in between coughing fits.

"He had two glasses of Port and was three sheets to the wind," explained Dow, grunting as he dragged Edgar's dead weight toward the door. "I told him to wait while I went to get him some coffee, but he went to the bar and found some himself… spiked with *rum*."

Thomas shuddered at the thought of this evil-sounding combination.

They got the door to Edgar's room open and dragged him inside. The unmistakable sound of vomiting was heard, followed by Dow loudly uttering a stream of profanity.

Inside, Edgar lied unconscious in the hotel room's bathtub as Dow gingerly peeled off his vomit-covered shirt.

"I'll need to borrow some of your clothes so I can get home," said Dow.

"Of course," Thomas replied.

Thomas examined Edgar, musing. "Do you think it's safe to leave him like this?"

"Damn it," Dow swore. "No. I have to get home to my wife… are you well enough to stay with him?"

Thomas sighed. "I suppose. I'll just sleep in here on his bed so I'll hear him if he wakes up."

Sunlight streamed in through the window onto the still-sleeping Thomas. A knock at the door startled Thomas awake. Disoriented by his unfamiliar surroundings, he stumbled over to the door.

Dow poked his head into the room.

"It's eleven-thirty. Did he make his meeting with the…" Dow broke off the moment he saw Edgar. "Oh my God."

He rushed into the room. The two men tried to wake Edgar up, repeatedly calling his name. When that failed, they tried to slap him awake. His skin was cadaverous and clammy. They shared a look of panic.

Finally, Edgar startled the bejesus out of both of them by coughing back to life.

He groaned. He looked around, confused, before sitting bolt upright in a panic.

"My meeting with the President!" he yelled, attempting to scramble out of the bathtub.

Thomas said gently, "It's eleven-thirty, Edgar."

"No…" Edgar sank down into the bathtub, his head in his hands.

WASHINGTON, March 12, 1843.

DEAR SIR. — I deem it to be my bounden duty to write you this hurried letter in relation to our mutual friend E. A. P.

He arrived here a few days since. On the first evening he seemed somewhat excited, having been overpersuaded to take some Port wine.

On the second day he kept pretty steady, but since then he has been, at intervals, quite unreliable.

He exposes himself here to those who may injure him very much with the President, and thus prevents us from doing for him what we wish to do and what we can do if he is himself again in Philadelphia. He does not understand the ways of politicians, nor the manner of dealing with them to advantage. How should he? Mr. Thomas is not well and cannot go home with Mr. P. My business and the health of my family will prevent me from so doing.

Under all the circumstances of the case, I think it advisable for you to come on and see him safely back to his home. Mrs. Poe is in a bad state of health, and I charge you, as you have a soul to be saved, to say not one word to her about him until he arrives with you. I shall expect you or an answer to this letter by return of mail.

Should you not come, we will see him on board the cars bound to Phila., but we fear he might be detained in Baltimore and not be out of harm's way.

I do this under a solemn responsibility. Mr. Poe has the highest order of intellect, and I cannot bear that he should be the sport of senseless creatures who, like oysters, keep sober, and gape and swallow everything.

I think your good judgment will tell you what course you ought to pursue in this matter, and I cannot think it will be necessary to let him know that I have written you this letter; but I cannot suffer him to injure himself here without giving you this warning.

Yours respectfully,

J. E. Dow.
To THOMAS C. CLARKE, Esq., Philadelphia, Pa.
(15)

Edgar stepped off the train, unshaven and disheveled, to see a grim, disappointed Muddy waiting for him. She surveyed him calmly, wordlessly communicating her disapproval. They walked home in silence. Edgar hung his head.

Virginia, despite being ill and weak, leapt up as the front door opened, so happy to have her husband back home and excited to hear good news.

Muddy silently, gravely entered and Virginia's smile turned to mild concern, then major concern once she saw Edgar. He dropped his luggage, walked over to her, looked into her eyes and shook his head. He fell to his knees and wrapped his arms around her waist. She closed her eyes and slowly, solemnly nodded her full understanding of exactly what had happened. She gently laid her hands on his head.

THE DOLLAR NEWSPAPER

Philadelphia, PA   *June 14, 1843*

Early after the first of June, we placed in the hands of the "Committee of Decision" all the stories which had reached us pursuant to our offer of premiums, and hoped to be able in the present number of our paper to publish their award, announcing all the premiums. The temporary indisposition of one of the Committee, and the necessary absence of another from town for a few days, have precluded them from concluding their labours as they expected. They have not, however, been idle, and inform us that they have gone over all the stories presented to them, and have awarded the *first prize* of ONE HUNDRED DOLLARS to "THE GOLD BUG," which we find, on examination of the private notes sent us, and which no one of the members of the Committee has seen, was written by Edgar A. Poe, Esq., of this city — and a capital story the Committee pronounce it to be.

THE DOLLAR NEWSPAPER

Philadelphia, PA   *June 28, 1843*

DON'T BE DISAPPOINTED — Those who, by delay, were last week disappointed in obtaining a copy of "The Dollar Newspaper," in consequence of the large supply having been early exhausted, will take care this week to call early and secure a copy. It contains the conclusion of that excellent prize story, "The Gold-Bug," the merits of which we spoke fully last week. The public demand for the paper bears out all that we have said of the Tale. All who have read it through, so far as we have heard it spoken of, pronounce it superior to any American production that they ever before read. The interest given to the story in working up the mystery to the point at which it stopped last week, is successfully maintained to the conclusion in elucidating it.

A hundred dollars was enough for the Poes to pay off all their debts and start over. New York City remained the center of the publishing world, so they decided to give it a second shot.

Happy and hopeful, Edgar and Virginia rode the train to New York. As they talked, joked and laughed like old times, Edgar noticed something out the window and excitedly pointed it out to Virginia… A veritable swarm of hot air balloons! Virginia's jaw dropped with delight and together they animatedly, excitedly watched them until they were no longer in sight.

Exhausted by a long day of travel, Edgar and Virginia trudged wearily down the shabby hallway of the boarding house in which they'd rented a room. The wallpaper was faded and the wainscoting needed a fresh coat of paint, but it was inexpensive. Edgar, finding their room number, gratefully dropped all of their luggage in front of the door, opened it and shoved the luggage inside, tearing his pants on a nail that jutted out of the doorway.

"Shit," he cursed.

He flopped on the bed, which though lumpy, felt good on his aching body. Virginia plopped next to him, untying her bonnet and unbuttoning her coat. She sighed, happy to be home. Home was wherever they could lie together, just like this.

"I'll start unpacking in a second," he breathed, his eyes closed.

Virginia smiled, rolled onto her side, wrapped her arm around him and kissed him.

"While you do that, I'll repair your pants," she giggled.

Laughing, he unbuttoned them, took them off and handed him to her. In his underwear, he tiredly unpacked, putting their clothes away and placing the few trinkets and other belongings that they'd been able to bring while Virginia set about stitching the rip in his pants, watching him busily dart around the room. She smiled and set his pants aside.

"I have this feeling of déjà vu," she said, slyly smiling.

"Oh?" he asked.

"Here we are once again, in New York, alone, and you're not wearing any pants," she giggled.

Edgar laughed and gave her an intrigued look.

"I don't know… do you think you're strong enough for…?" he asked.

Virginia stood up, walked over to him, wrapped her arms around his neck and kissed him.

"I haven't so much as coughed all day. And I haven't had any fever this week," she whispered, looking intently into his eyes.

He gazed back at her for a second before shutting his eyes and kissing her, as they sank down onto the bed.

The next morning, sunlight shone through the faded curtains onto the still-sleeping Edgar and Virginia, who lied tangled up in each other's arms, wrapped naked together in a sheet. Virginia opened her eyes and smiled. Her eyes widened and she quickly sat up.

"Eddy!" she said, "I smell pancakes!"

He stretched and yawned. His stomach growled audibly.

"Oh God, is that bacon?" he said, wide awake and *hungry*.

They got dressed as quickly as they could and ran downstairs.

As they reached the bottom of the stairs, they saw the dining room table, piled high with the most sumptuous breakfast. The round, cheerful proprietress beckoned them to help themselves. They wasted no time, diving into chairs and digging in.

They ate like they'd never eaten before. Once thoroughly full, they laughed hysterically as they laboriously made their way back upstairs, so stuffed they could hardly walk.

New-York, Sunday Morning April 7. just after breakfast.

My dear Muddy,

We have just this minute done breakfast, and I now sit down to write you about everything. I can't pay for the letter, because the P.O. won't be open to-day. —— In the first place, we arrived safe at Walnut St wharf. The driver wanted to make me pay a dollar, but I wouldn't. Then I had to pay a boy a levy to put the trunks in the baggage car. In the meantime I took Sis in the Depot Hotel. It was only a quarter past 6, and we had to wait till 7. We saw the Ledger & Times — nothing in either — a few words of no account in the Chronicle. — We started in good spirits, but did not get here until nearly 3 o'clock. We went in the cars to Amboy about 40 miles from N. York, and then took the steamboat the rest of the way. — Sissy coughed none at all. When we got to the wharf it was raining hard. I left her on board the boat, after putting the trunks in the Ladies' Cabin, and set off to buy an umbrella and look for a boarding-house. I met a man selling umbrellas and bought one for 62 cents. Then I went up Greenwich St and soon found a boarding-house. It is just before you get to Cedar St on the West side going up — the left hand side. It has brown stone steps, with a porch with brown pillars. "Morrison" is the name on the

door. I made a bargain in a few minutes and then got
a hack and went for Sis. I was not gone more than
1/2 an hour, and she was quite astonished to see me
back so soon. She didn't expect me for an hour.
There were 2 other ladies waiting on board — so she
was'nt very lonely. — When we got to the house we
had to wait about 1/2 an hour before the room... The
house is old & looks buggy... The landlady is a nice
chatty ol... gave us the back room on th... night &
day & attendance, for 7 $ — the cheapest board I
ever knew, taking into consideration the central
situation and the living. I wish Kate could see it —
she would faint. Last night, for supper, we had the
nicest tea you ever drank, strong & hot — wheat
bread & rye bread — cheese — tea-cakes (elegant) a
great dish (2 dishes) of elegant ham, and 2 of cold
veal piled up like a mountain and large slices — 3
dishes of the cakes and, and every thing in the
greatest profusion. No fear of starving here. The
landlady seemed as if she couldn't press us enough,
and we were at home directly. Her husband is living
with her — a fat good-natured old soul. There are 8
or 10 boarders — 2 or 3 of them ladies — 2 servants.
— For breakfast we had excellent-flavored coffee, hot
& strong — not very clear & no great deal of cream —
veal cutlets, elegant ham & eggs & nice bread and
butter. I never sat down to a more plentiful or a nicer
breakfast. I wish you could have seen the eggs —
and the great dishes of meat. I ate the first hearty
breakfast I have eaten since I left our little home. Sis
is delighted, and we are both in excellent spirits. She
has coughed hardly any and had no night sweat. She
is now busy mending my pants which I tore against a
nail. I went out last night and bought a skein of silk,
a skein of thread, & 2 buttons, a pair of slippers & a

tin pan for the stove. The fire kept in all night. — We have now got 4 $ and a half left. Tomorrow I am going to try & borrow 3 $ — so that I may have a fortnight to go upon. I feel in excellent spirits & haven't drank a drop — so that I hope so to get out of trouble. The very instant I scrape together enough money I will sent it on. You can't imagine how much we both to miss you. Sissy had a hearty cry last night, because you and Catterina weren't here. We are resolved to get 2 rooms the first moment we can. In the meantime it is impossible we could be more comfortable or more at home than we are. — It looks as if it was going to clear up now. — Be sure and go to the P.O. & have my letters forwarded. As soon as I write Lowell's article, I will send it to you, & get you to get the money from Graham. Give our best loves to Catterina **(16)**

Edgar lied on the bed reading a book on mesmerism and taking notes in the margins. There was a knock at the door. Edgar looked up as Virginia set her knitting aside to answer it.

"Muddy!" she exclaimed, as Muddy entered, carrying a fat tortoiseshell cat. "I'm so happy to see you!"

"Catterina!" exclaimed Edgar, as the cat hopped down from Muddy's arms and trotted over to him, purring.

"This place will do nicely," nodded Muddy, examining the room.

Edgar petted the cat and smooched it on the head. "How much do we have left from the sale of our furniture, after your trip?"

"Twelve dollars," Muddy breathed, plopping into a chair with an audible "oof."

"Do you have any prospects?" she asked him.

"I've just written a tale that should cause a sensation," he grinned.

Sun Office

April 13, 10:00 AM

ASTOUNDING NEWS!

BY EXPRESS VIA NORFOLK!

THE

ATLANTIC CROSSED

IN

THREE DAYS!

SIGNAL TRIUMPH

OF

MR. MONCK MASON'S

FLYING

MACHINE!!!

Arrival at Sullivan's Island, near Charleston, S. C., of Mr. Mason, Mr. Robert Holland, Mr. Henson, Mr. Harrison Ainsworth, and four others, in the STEERING BALLOON **"VICTORIA**," AFTER A PASSAGE OF **SEVENTY-FIVE HOURS FROM LAND TO LAND**. FULL PARTICULARS OF THE **VOYAGE**!!! **(17)**

Riding high from the success of "The Gold Bug" and "The Balloon-Hoax," Edgar nervously prepared to give his first lecture in New York. Virginia straightened his collar and tied his cravat, then stood back and inspected him, nodding appreciatively. Satisfied with his appearance, she hugged him and kissed him.

"Good luck tonight," she smiled, her arms draped around his neck.

"With you as my good luck charm, I can't go wrong," he grinned back at her, kissing her once more before heading for the door, manuscript in hand.

As he touched the doorknob, Virginia coughed. He stopped dead in his tracks, icy goosebumps covering his entire body. He turned around slowly, praying that he wouldn't see what he feared… But Virginia was fine. She smiled at him, reassuringly waving the cough off. Edgar forced a smile back, which turned to a frown as he noticed a raven sitting on the windowsill, cawing. He contemplated it quizzically for a moment, genuinely unsettled.

"I'm fine, darling," Virginia said, sweetly, "Go, you can't be late for your first lecture!"

Edgar stood at the podium, confident but somewhat jittery, repeatedly checking his pocket watch. Covered in a fine dew of perspiration, he took a deep breath, tried not to notice the number of people in the audience, arranged his papers one final time and began.

The standing-room-only audience hung on his every word. He animatedly walked around the stage, passionately hammering his points home, his slight Southern accent popping through.

"An important condition of man's immortal nature is thus, plainly, the sense of the Beautiful. This it is which ministers to his delight in the manifold forms and colors and sounds and sentiments amid which he exists. And, just as the eyes of Amaryllis are repeated in the mirror, or the living lily in the lake, so is the mere *record* of these forms and colors and sounds and sentiments — so is their mere oral or written repetition a duplicate source of delight. But this repetition is not Poesy. He who shall merely sing with whatever rapture, in however harmonious strains, or with however vivid a truth of imitation, of the sights and sounds which greet him in common with all mankind — he, we say, has yet failed to prove his divine title. There is still a longing unsatisfied, which he has been impotent to fulfil. There is still a thirst unquenchable, which to allay he has shown us no crystal springs. This burning thirst belongs to the *immortal* essence of man's nature. It is equally a consequence and an indication of his perennial life. It is the desire of the moth for the star. It is not the mere appreciation of the beauty before us. It is a wild effort to reach the beauty above. It is a forethought of the loveliness to come. It is a passion to be satiated by no sub-lunary sights, or sounds, or sentiments, and the soul thus athirst strives to allay its fever in futile efforts at *creation*. Inspired with a prescient ecstasy of the beauty beyond the grave, it struggles by multiform novelty of combination among the things and thoughts of Time, to anticipate some portion of that loveliness whose very elements, perhaps, appertain solely to Eternity. And the result of such effort, on the part of souls fittingly constituted, is alone what mankind have agreed to denominate Poetry." **(18)**

With that, he finished, triumphant. The audience waited a moment in case there were more. Once sure he had finished, they rose for a rousing standing ovation.

Whistling, a spring in his step, Edgar walked home, encouraged and delighted with his success and positively bursting with excitement to share it with his wife. He strode up the stairs two at a time and energetically walked down the hall to their room. Halfway down, he stopped as if he'd been shot. The door to their room hung open. From inside, he heard Virginia wheezing and coughing. He ran the rest of the way to their door and into their room, his heart pounding.

A doctor attended to Virginia, who lied on the bed, pale, gasping for air, with blood caked around her mouth. Relief appeared in her panicked eyes as she saw her husband was home. He ran to her, knelt down and took her hand. She clutched his hand tightly, unable to talk, as tears

sprang from her eyes.

By day, Edgar feverishly wrote reviews for the papers and magazines while Muddy went out and tried her best to get them sold. He burned the candle at both ends to scrape enough together to pay the rent, feed his family and buy Virginia's medicine, but he couldn't have slept if he'd wanted to, as Virginia coughed night and day, and shook with the terrible fever and night sweats of tuberculosis. Every night, he nursed her and wrote.

Her every shuddering breath chilled him to the bone. His constant worry for her created lines and furrows in his face. Lack of sleep and insufficient food rendered him gaunt. Anxiously, he wet a washcloth in a basin, wrung it out and laid it on Virginia's forehead.

"There, there, darling," he whispered, "This will help cool you down."

Virginia nodded. He looked at her sorrowfully and lovingly, took her hand in his and kissed it.

"Try to get some sleep," he said, gently, "Rest will help you get better." She nodded again, forced a smile, and continuing to cough uncontrollably, rolled over. Edgar returned to his desk and by candlelight, worked on his new poem: "The Raven."

"The Raven" was reprinted over and over, selling out newspapers and causing Edgar's presence to be in high demand at New York's literary *salons.* He read "The Raven" nightly to packed parlors, as all who were present sat silent and transfixed, hanging on his every word. The ladies in particular were quite taken with the handsome young poet. A tiny, frail, bird-like woman who sat in front every night gazed adoringly at him, every breath causing her small bosom to heave as tears stood in her eyes. Other attendees saw right through her and regarded her with eye-rolls and derision, but she was past caring. She was in love with him, she wanted him and she didn't give a damn about much else.

Once he finished with his recitation and the applause died down, Fanny Osgood decided tonight was the night. She couldn't hold it in any longer, she would make her move.

She flitted over to him, delicately weaving her way through the crowd, and timidly approached him.

"Mr. Poe, your recitation of "The Raven" was so magical! It's so musical, I could positively dance to it!" she breathed.

Edgar nodded and smiled cordially. "Thank you, Fanny, I'm so glad you enjoyed it," he replied.

He met and greeted other guests, shaking hands and graciously accepting their praise. Fanny hung around until she saw another opening.

"I also want to thank you for your review of my latest volume," she gushed. "Having the praise of a critic of your caliber means everything!"

"There are quite a few pieces in it with real merit," Edgar replied, formally.

Another woman hovering nearby saw her opportunity to wiggle through.

"Mr. Poe, my name is Elizabeth Ellet, I was wondering if you've gotten my letters… You must not have, since you haven't resp—" she stammered.

"My husband wants to talk to you about painting your portrait," Fanny interrupted, boldly taking Edgar by the arm and dragging him to the opposite side of the room. Edgar smiled apologetically and nodded cordially at Mrs. Ellet.

Her initial surprise and embarrassment switched quickly to

jealous rage. Seething, her cheeks flushed bright red.

Virginia sat in bed, wheezing and fretfully reading a letter. Her cheeks pink with fever, her brows knit, she folded it up, tucked it into her bodice and swore. In the dark, she sat alone, coughing, waiting for her husband to come home. The dinner she'd saved for him sat cold on his desk. At last, the door opened and he tiptoed inside.

"Finally!" she wheezed, speaking haltingly, short of breath. "Welcome home. I saved you some dinner. Sorry it's cold."

"Oh, thank you, I'm starving," he said, dropping his cloak onto his chair and kicking off his shoes. He leaned in to kiss her, but she turned away.

"Sis?" he asked.

"I hope tomorrow won't be such a long day," she said, her voice breaking. "I missed you."

"I'm sorry, darling," he said. "The price of success. 'The Raven' has me quite in demand at the moment."

"Those salons don't even *pay* you," she said, angrily.

"I know," he sighed. "And the nine dollars I got paid for "The Raven" is long gone. I can only hope that all this rubbing elbows with literary socialites will lead to more work."

"Well," she glowered, "It does seem to have earned you some *ardent* admirers."

Edgar was puzzled. "Oh?"

"I'm getting the most *fascinating* letters from one Mrs. Elizabeth Ellet," she said through a sob.

"What?" he demanded.

Virginia angrily jutted her arm out from the blanket and handed him the letter.

"Yes, she seems to think you're having an affair with Fanny Osgood," Virginia continued.

"You have to know that there's no—" he said.

"*Of course not.* I know your soul. I know you'd *never* be unfaithful to me," she said, crying. He got in bed next to her.

"All those literary society people, they're so *horrible*," she cried. "Idiots and hangers on, every last one of them fake. Jealous vipers who fear and try to stamp out anything that's *real*!" She sobbed into his vest. He held her tightly, looking heavenward.

"You're *famous*," she swore. "But for what? We still have no money. And now whores are publicly throwing themselves at you and I know you'd never be tempted by a single one of them, but it's embarrassing! And now they're trying to cause us problems at *home*. And that's where I draw the line. Get me out of here! Get me out of this stinking, rat-infested hellhole!"

She buried her face in his chest and let all her frustration and rage out in a torrent of tears. He sobbed with her, the two of them holding and rocking each other in the moonlight.

The next morning, Edgar dressed. As he tied his cravat, there was a knock at the door. At this early hour, he assumed it was Muddy. He flung the door open with a cheerful, "Good morning, Muddy!"

But it wasn't Muddy. It was a very sullen, hostile Fanny Osgood. From bed, Virginia glowered at her.

"Uh… can I help you?" asked Edgar, forcing cordiality.

"Mrs. Ellet has asked me to retrieve her letters from you," Fanny coldly demanded.

"Oh, *really*," said Edgar sarcastically. He lost his composure and angrily fired back, "Tell Mrs. Ellet that if she put as much into her poetry as she does into her poison pen letters, she'd actually have a career worth speaking of. She can look after her *own* letters."

With that, Edgar slammed the door in her face. Virginia covered her mouth in shock and laughed involuntarily. She had never seen her husband this pissed off before.

Edgar walked purposefully past a row of brownstones with a small package of letters in his hand. He scanned the address numbers for the one he wanted and finding it, strode up to the door, placed the letters on the doorstep, rang the doorbell and stalked briskly away.

Moments later, the door opened. Elizabeth Ellet looked around, confused, trying to see who rang the doorbell but it was no use. Edgar was out of sight. Finally, she looked down and saw the letters. She quickly snatched them up, and seeing what they were, she went back inside and slammed the door behind her. She screamed with animal fury and threw them into the blazing fireplace, where they were immediately and completely engulfed.

Edgar headed home after his annoying errand. As he neared his boarding house, a fat, brutish man with a menacing mien began following him. Closely. Threateningly. Just as Edgar noticed his presence, the man lunged at him and grabbed him by the collar.

"Give me my sister's letters, you son of a bitch!" he growled.

Edgar stammered, "What the hell are you talking about?"

"You claim to have some letters, " the man grunted, "that you say she better look after."

This confused Edgar for a moment, before he realized who this man must be.

"I don't have them… I've already returned them! I placed them on her doorstep half an hour ago!" he stammered.

"Bullshit!" the men yelled, and punched Edgar in the face, knocking him to the ground. The punch caused a cut above Edgar's left eyebrow, which bled profusely.

"I'm telling you that I don't!" Edgar yelled. "She has them back as of half an hour ago!"

"Liar!" the man roared. He grabbed Edgar by the collar again. "You're gonna bring those letters back to her by sundown, or *you and me are gonna have a duel.*" He let go of Edgar's collar and stomped away. Edgar wiped blood from his brow, his hand shaking.

A doctor stitched up the cut above Edgar's eyebrow.

"Almost done," the doctor said. "What did a man of letters like you get into a fistfight about, anyway?"

Edgar sighed. "There's this woman…"

"Ah," said the doctor, with a knowing nod.

"No, it's not like that…" Edgar explained.

"Listen…" Edgar continued. "I need you to do me a favor and write a letter for me, just a brief note will do."

"Alright," answered the doctor quizzically, tugging the thread taut as he performed the last stitch.

"I'd like you to write a note, addressed to Mrs. Elizabeth Ellet, in which you declare me to be temporarily insane."

"Whaaaat?" the doctor asked, incredulous.

"Yes. Tell her I was temporarily insane when I made the allegation about the letters," Edgar explained.

"Alright…" the doctor replied, shrugging his shoulders.

"Thank you," Edgar sighed, relieved. "If you could please deliver it to her this evening, you will likely be saving my life."

Edgar, despondent and defeated, quietly entered his room. Inside, he found Virginia sleeping. He admired her for a moment, taking in how angelic she looked. Finding her here, at home as always, beautiful as always, renewed him. She was the one constant in his life. No matter what, he had her. He could withstand anything for her, with her at his side.

Quietly, he took off his shoes and his cloak. He was about to get in bed next to her when he noticed a letter on his desk. It was addressed to him, from Virginia Poe – dated February 14th, 1846. "Valentine's Day!" he gasped. In all the chaos of the last few days, he'd forgotten. He quietly, carefully unsealed the letter and read.

"Ever with thee I wish to roam —
Dearest my life is thine.
Give me a cottage for my home
And a rich old cypress vine,
Removed from the world with its
sin and care
And the tattling of many
tongues.
Love alone shall guide us when
we are there —
Love shall heal my weakened
lungs;
And Oh, the tranquil hours we'll spend,
Never wishing that others may
see!
Perfect ease we'll enjoy, without
thinking to lend
Ourselves to the world and its
glee —
Ever peaceful and blissful we'll
be." **(19)**

Tears rolled down his face as he read, growing into a

sob as he reached the bottom. He sobbed quietly into his

sleeve, trying not to wake her. With some effort, he

collected himself and smiled wistfully, watching her sleep.

Edgar walked briskly through the streets of Manhattan, manuscript in hand, another day spent trying to get an article sold to put some food on the table. The Raven descended from a nearby lamppost and began to fly a few feet behind him. As he walked, additional ravens hopped down from buildings and trees, one by one, joining the first raven to form a malevolent murder of crows. Like the anthropomorphic Raven of his poem, they eerily seemed able to talk, and they tormented him, chasing him, hurling insults, angry jabs, puns on his name and other epithets that had been published in the papers as a result of the scandal that Mrs. Ellet had caused.

"Infamous!"

"Drunk!"

"Madman!"

"Insane!"

"Depraved!"

As their aggression intensified, he quickened his pace, his heart pounding. Desperate to escape the growing, teeming cloud of negativity, he broke into a full run.

Carrying Virginia in his arms, on a bright, sunny morning, the air cold, the grass covered with dew, Edgar walked down a rugged country path.

"You're really not going to tell me where you're taking me?" Virginia smiled, wheezing weakly, her head balanced securely on his shoulder, her arms draped around his neck.

"That would spoil the surprise," Edgar grinned.

He hiked up onto a hill, rounded a gentle curve and stopped. Virginia lifted her head from his shoulder, looked up and gasped.

There in front of them was a cozy, quaint country cottage, surrounded by flowering cherry trees in full, magnificent bloom. She turned to Edgar with tears in her eyes, speechless.

"You asked me to give you a cottage for your home," whispered Edgar.

A gentle wind blew, showering the Poes with a snow of cherry blossoms.

Edgar and Muddy unpacked as Virginia sat on a simple, bare straw bed, petting the cat, which purred on her lap. The cottage was rustic and sparsely furnished, but to her it was a palace. Despite her frailty, she smiled delightedly as she watched Edgar and Muddy put their things away and make it home.

"I'm going into the city later," Muddy said, unrolling a rug. "I'll do my best to get your article sold."

Edgar nodded.

"Are you sure you don't want to come along and visit the magazines yourself?" she tentatively asked.

Edgar, shelving books, looked out the window at New York City off in the distance. The Murder of Crows circled ominously, swirling above it like bats out of Hell.

"No… I can't," he replied, swallowing hard. "I feel ill."

Edgar wrote by candlelight, as Virginia coughed violently in bed; body-wracking, violent hacking. His hand shook. He tried to ignore it. His stomach growled audibly. He looked over at Virginia, then back at his manuscript. He sighed. He got up, went to the kitchen, rummaged through all the empty cabinets and drawers, before finding the last of their bread, a mere rind, in the bread box. Hungrily, gratefully, he ate it. The guilt of eating the very last of their food gnawed at him, but he didn't have a choice. He went over to the fire and tended it, stoking the smoldering coals. His eyes wide and filled with high-wire anxiety, he stared into the anemic fire and cringed with Virginia's every cough.

Gaunt, haggard, keyed-up and twitchy, Edgar dressed in his best suit, which was patched and worn. Virginia dozed, feverish and miserable, as Muddy wrung her hands.

"Are you sure there's any point in doing this?" Muddy asked timidly, as if she were poking a bear.

"The only way to stop the slander and clear my name is to sue!" Edgar snapped back, short and defensive.

"Alright…" Muddy sighed with resignation. "Are you sure you can manage going into the city alone? Or should I come along?"

"No, someone needs to stay here to watch Virginia. I'll

be fine on my own," he replied, shutting the front door

behind him.

At a country bar, Edgar drank alone. He added one more shot to his tab before stumbling out the door.

He walked unsteadily toward the train station. In the distance, the Murder of Crows vibrated with negativity over the city, bigger and darker than ever. He eyed it with dread, took a deep breath and kept walking.

Night. Muddy dabbed Virginia's forehead with a wash cloth as Virginia, wraith-like and near death, shook and perspired with the terrible night sweats of tuberculosis. A knock at the door startled Muddy nearly out of her skin.

She set the washcloth down, went to the door and opened it. She disappeared outside for a moment before re-entering with a note in her hand, saying "Thank you" to the messenger. She closed the door behind her, opened the note, scanned to the bottom and sighed with relief. She brought it over to Virginia.

"It's from Eddy," she told her.

Virginia nodded, relieved. She had been worried that

her Eddy was uncharacteristically late in coming home.

Muddy handed the note to Virginia, and Virginia read.

My Dear Heart, My dear Virginia! our Mother will
explain to you why I stay away from you this night. I
trust the interview I am promised, will result in some
substantial good for me, for your dear sake, and hers
— Keep up your heart in all hopefulness, and trust
yet a little longer — In my last great disappointment,
I should have lost my courage *but for you* — my little
darling wife you are my *greatest* and *only* stimulus
now, to battle with this uncongenial, unsatisfactory
and ungrateful life — I shall be with you tomorrow
P.M. and be assured until I see you, I will keep in
loving remembrance your *last words* and your fervant
prayer!

Sleep well and may God grant you a peaceful
summer, with your devoted

Edgar **(20)**

She smiled, tears rolling down her face, and shut her

eyes, comforted by her husband's note.

The fire low and frost on the window, Edgar's breath was visible as he worked on "The Cask of Amontillado" by candlelight amid Virginia's violent coughing. Suddenly, her coughing turned to sounds of drowning… liquid gasping and multi-toned wheezing. Edgar jumped out of his chair and ran to her bedside.

"Darling?" he croaked, lifting her up in his arms. "Darling?!"

Virginia, wearing his cloak as a blanket, couldn't answer him. Her glassy eyes rolled back in her head. She couldn't breathe.

"No. No, no, no…" Edgar cried, holding her to his chest, rocking her, brushing her hair out of her face.

"Breathe, Sissy," he said gently, his voice breaking. "Please… breathe."

Her hands clutched his shoulders in a death-grip. She wheezed, gurgled, and finally, after a few terrifying moments of silence, began to take shuddering but regular breaths. Edgar watched her intensely as she took another breath… then another… and another. Exhausted but relieved, he held her tightly, cradling her head to his chest, and stared into the dying embers of the fire.

Edgar lied in bed next to Virginia, closely watching her sleep. Sleep deprivation had rendered him haggard and he too now had a terrible cough. Muddy walked in the front door, carrying a newspaper. She headed directly over to Edgar and Virginia before even taking off her coat and scarf.

"Edgar!" she said, handing him the paper, "We're saved. Your illness has been announced in the papers and a collection is being taken up on your behalf."

Edgar looked at her, bewildered and horrified. He tried to protest this humiliating idea, but just gave himself a terrible coughing fit. Virginia stirred and opened her eyes. Edgar, finding the article, read aloud.

"It is said that Edgar A. Poe is lying dangerously ill with the brain fever, and that his wife is in the last stages of consumption – they are without money and without friends." **(21)**

Edgar stopped, stung. Virginia began to cry. He took

her hand to comfort her and tried to read on, but was once

again seized by a convulsive fit of coughing. He handed the

paper to Muddy, gesturing to her to continue reading.

"Mr. Poe was engaged with us in the editorship of a daily paper, we think, for about six months. A more considerate, quiet, talented, and gentlemanlike associate than he was for the whole of that time, we could not have wished... He left us, by his own wish alone, and it was one day soon after that we first saw him in the state to which we refer. He came into our office with his usual gait and manner and with no symptoms of ordinary intoxication, he talked like a man insane. Perfectly self-possessed in all other respects, his brain and tongue were evidently beyond his control. We learned afterwards that the least stimulus — a single glass of wine — would produce this effect upon Mr. Poe, and that rarely as these instances of easy aberration of caution and mind occurred, he was liable to them, and while under their influence, voluble and personally self-possessed, but neither sane nor responsible. Now Mr. Poe very possibly may not be willing to consent to even this admission of any infirmity. He has little or no memory of them afterwards, we understand.

But public opinion unqualifiedly holds him blamable for what he has said and done under such excitements, and while a call is made in a public paper for aid, it looks like doing him a timely service to, at least, partially exonerate him." **(22)**

Remembering his recent trip into the city, Edgar covered his face with his hands in humiliated disbelief as Muddy and Virginia shared a look of mortified shock.

Edgar and Virginia dozed in bed, nestled together under Edgar's cloak, their only source of warmth. Muddy paced, her eyes darting frequently to the front window. Finally, she saw someone step onto the porch and threw open the front door.

"Thank you so much for coming, Mrs. Shew," said Muddy.

Mrs. Marie Louise Shew, a rotund, well-dressed woman with a saintly visage, entered the cottage, carrying a doctor's bag. She looked around, making a cursory inspection, and quickly sized the situation up.

"Oh, my," she said, in a sweet, musical voice. "This won't do at all."

Mrs. Shew laid a lush blanket over Edgar and Virginia, who now lied on a proper feather bed covered in fresh, new linens instead of a bare, straw mattress. Mrs. Shew stuck a thermometer into Edgar's mouth, grabbed his wrist and felt for his pulse.

"You may still feel awful," she said, "but you're better than before. Being kept warm enough will help you recover."

Edgar weakly nodded his gratitude.

Mrs. Shew went to the other side of the bed to tend to Virginia. Muddy approached Edgar, wringing her hands.

"Eddy… I know what you're going to say, but… you've received a lucrative proposition from the poetess Stella Lewis," she said.

Edgar wrinkled his nose in disgust at the word "poetess" being used to describe this particular literary society irritant.

"She is offering *a hundred dollars* for you to write a favorable notice of her volume of poetry…" Muddy continued, trailing off.

Edgar glowered.

"It's a hundred dollars, Edgar…" Muddy plaintively whispered.

Edgar swore around the thermometer, but finally, rolling his eyes, nodded his consent.

The kitchen stocked with plenty of food, a freshly baked loaf of bread still steaming from the oven, Muddy cleaned up the kitchen after dinner. Vials of medicine lined the windowsill next to Virginia's bed, where Edgar sat, intently watching her breathe, like a mother watching a newborn. Her chest shuddered with every shallow, noisy breath.

Virginia weakly turned and looked into his eyes. She frowned. She knew she didn't have long and was worried about how Edgar would handle life without her. Tears rolled down her cheeks. She tried to say something, but couldn't. She could only cough and weep weakly, wordlessly.

Edgar leapt into bed next to her to comfort her.

"Hey, now…" he said, kissing her forehead. "Don't you fret. Relax, Sissy… Relax."

She gazed up at him and listened.

"You'll get better," he said, stroking her face. "You have to. We have a lot to do."

At this, she cried harder. He gently wiped her tears away and stroked her hair.

"Remember? We're going on vacation soon. We're going to take a hot air balloon to outer space. We'll take the very latest, the very best balloon, with all the finest luxury accommodations," he said.

Virginia couldn't help but smile amid her pain and fear.

"We'll stop by the moon and say hello to Hans Pfaall," he grinned. "It's the least we can do, I *did* leave him there, after all."

At this, Virginia giggled, feebly but audibly. She nodded, soothed by this tale that he had spun just for her. She snuggled into his chest, shut her eyes and fell asleep, the same way she'd fallen asleep every night for the last eleven years. He kissed the top of her head, holding her tightly, and shut his eyes, too, laying his head on the pillow.

Sun cascaded in through the frosty window onto the still-sleeping Edgar and Virginia. The sunlight fell onto Edgar's eyelids and woke him up. He opened his eyes, saw his wife cradled in his arms and smiled. He kissed her forehead, then panicked.

"Sis?? SISSY?!" he screamed.

Edgar lifted Virginia's body up and her head lolled back unnaturally. He irrationally tried to feel for a pulse in her neck and broke into body-wracking sobs, clutching Virginia's limp body tightly, screaming his grief.

A young priest officiated Virginia's sparsely-attended funeral.

Edgar, numb, catatonic, helplessly watched as Virginia's casket lowered into the ground.

Curled into the fetal position, Edgar lied on Virginia's snow-covered grave, his shirt half-buttoned, wearing no coat, no shoes. Frost on his mustache, tears frozen to his face, he sobbed, shivered and talked to his wife through chattering teeth, as a blizzard slowly buried him.

"Oh, dear Jesus," Mrs. Shew cried, approaching him.

The priest that officiated Virginia's funeral scooped Edgar up into his arms like a baby as Mrs. Shew threw a blanket over him. Against the wind, they carried him home.

Edgar, haggard and thin, his face covered in three weeks' beard, stared out into space at his desk. He grabbed his pen, and at the bottom of a manuscript of his poem, "Eulalie," he wrote:

> "Deep in earth my love is lying
> And I must weep alone." **(23)**

He set his pen down and resumed blankly staring at the wall.

On the front porch of the cottage, on a clear, cold, blue-sky morning, Edgar packed some apples, a notebook and a pencil into a satchel. He took a deep breath and headed down the stairs, into the prismatic morning fog. Agilely, he walked through the woods, filling his lungs with fresh, clean air. The fog began to lift as the sun rose completely, gleaming through the trees in bright shafts. Reaching the shore, he stopped.

On an island a few hundred yards out was a beautiful lighthouse. The only building on the island, it stood majestically, sunlight reflecting brightly off of its lens. As Edgar caught his breath and tasted the salt air, a man and a huge, happy Newfoundland dog emerged from the lighthouse's front door. The man threw a large stick and the dog expertly, athletically ran and caught it perfectly in his mouth, splashing in the surf. "That's it, Neptune!" the man laughed.

The man sat on a big rock, opened a book and read as Neptune splashed and played.

"Pure solitude, but for a delightful dog," smiled Edgar. "That would be heaven. Heaven."

He stripped off his shirt, rolled up the cuffs of his pants, dove in and went for a leisurely swim, floating on his back, contentedly basking in the sunlight. Satisfied, he climbed out, hungrily ate his apples and lied down to rest, using his satchel as a pillow. He took out his notebook and pencil, and, feeling wrung out, exercised, healthy and good, he wrote.

"Six years ago, a wife, whom I loved as no man
ever loved before, ruptured a blood-vessel in singing.
Her life was despaired of. I took leave of her forever &
underwent all the agonies of her death. She
recovered partially and I again hoped. At the end of a
year the vessel broke again — I went through
precisely the same scene. Again in about a year
afterward. Then again — again — again & even once
again at varying intervals. Each time I felt all the
agonies of her death — and at each accession of the
disorder I loved her more dearly & clung to her life
with more desperate pertinacity. But I am
constitutionally sensitive — nervous in a very
unusual degree. I became insane, with long intervals
of horrible sanity. During these fits of absolute
unconsciousness I drank, God only knows how often
or how much. As a matter of course, my enemies
referred the insanity to the drink rather than the
drink to the insanity. I had indeed, nearly abandoned
all hope of a permanent cure when I found one in the
death of my wife. This I can & do endure as becomes
a man — it was the horrible never-ending oscillation
between hope & despair which I could *not* longer
have endured without the total loss of reason. In the
death of what was my life, then, I receive a new but
— oh God! how melancholy an existence." **(24)**

Edgar, valise in hand, trunk at his feet, hugged Muddy goodbye on the cottage's porch. She dabbed tears from her eyes and straightened his collar and cravat.

"Are you sure you'll be alright?" she asked. "You look rather pale."

She placed her hand on his forehead.

"Edgar, you have a fever. Couldn't you rest tonight and start your lecture tour tomorrow?" she suggested.

"I'm fine, Muddy. Really. It's just a few days' work, and I'll be right back home before you know it," he smiled confidently.

Muddy wasn't so sure, but forced a nod of agreement.

Tired after a day of railway travel, Edgar lied in his hotel bed. It was very late and completely dark except for moonlight. He gazed out the window at the stars as he began to doze.

As he dropped off, a ghostlike female figure tiptoed into the room, wearing a gauzy, flowing, white nightgown, her long hair down. She climbed onto the bed and on top of him.

He gave no resistance as she kissed him. He kissed her hard, grasping the back of her head, pulling her closer. He yielded to her completely as she made love to him, her hair cascading around his face like a shimmering curtain. In ecstasy, he brushed her hair off of her face and saw that she was Virginia, his Virginia. Their passion intensified and he clutched her closer, closer.

He started awake. He looked around, confused. The room was empty, he was alone. It was only a dream. He rolled over and stared at the wall.

Deeply depressed, Edgar rode the train to Boston.

In a new hotel, he lied curled up on the bed, sobbing into his cloak, the one Virginia had used as a blanket, his face buried in it, his arms wrapped around it as if it were a person.

He stood up and looked in the mirror. He was a mess. He splashed some water on his face, smoothed his hair, threw on his cloak and walked out the door.

He walked briskly, trying to distract himself from his agony with the cool evening air. He saw a pharmacy that was still open, made a snap decision and went inside. On a nearby lamppost, the Raven cawed.

Inside, Edgar placed his order.

"Laudanum," he said hoarsely.

"How much?" asked the pharmacist.

Edgar didn't know anything about laudanum and had to stop and think.

"Two ounces," he guessed.

The pharmacist eyed him suspiciously but mixed up his order.

Tucking the laudanum into his cloak, Edgar left, walking with purpose back to his hotel.

Edgar wrote, falling apart emotionally with each verse.

"It was many and many a year ago,
In a kingdom by the sea
That a maiden there lived whom you may know
By the name of ANNABEL LEE;
And this maiden she lived with no other thought
Than to love and be loved by me.

I was a child and she was a child,
In this kingdom by the sea.
But we loved with a love that was more than love —
I and my ANNABEL LEE —
With a love that the wingèd seraphs of heaven
Coveted her and me.

And this was the reason that, long ago,
In this kingdom by the sea,
A wind blew out of a cloud, chilling
My beautiful ANNABEL LEE;
So that her highborn kinsmen came
And bore her away from me,
To shut her up in a sepulchre
In this kingdom by the sea.

The angels, not half so happy in heaven,
Went envying her and me —

Yes! — that was the reason (as all men know,
In this kingdom by the sea)
That the wind came out of the cloud by night,
Chilling and killing my ANNABEL LEE.

But our love it was stronger by far than the love
Of those who were older than we —
Of many far wiser than we —
And neither the angels in heaven above,
Nor the demons down under the sea,
Can ever dissever my soul from the soul
Of the beautiful ANNABEL LEE:

For the moon never beams, without bringing me
dreams
Of the beautiful ANNABEL LEE;
And the stars never rise but I feel the bright eyes
Of the beautiful ANNABEL LEE,
And so, all the night-tide, I lie down by the side
Of my darling — my darling — my life and my bride,
In her sepulchre there by the sea—
In her tomb by the sounding sea." **(25)**

He opened the bottle of laudanum and drank it,

grimacing at its bitterness. He stared at the wall, waiting for

it to take effect.

The room spun. His heart pounded hard in his ears,

getting slower and slower with each beat.

He stood up, panicking, a suicide who has thought better of dying, but who now realizes there may be no way back. There was a loud **tapping** at the window. He turned, not wanting to see what he knew was there, but unable to resist. There The Raven was, pecking hard on the window. In his drugged state, each peck was deafening, like a sledgehammer hitting metal. He bolted out the door as fast as he could.

Pale and drenched in sweat, he ran clumsily down the street as The Raven flew menacingly behind him. The laudanum's effect deepened and he could only stumble, weaving back and forth, as other pedestrians dodged him.

The gas lights developed streaks and tails. The night grew blurry. He fell to his knees and vomited convulsively, coughing and gasping as people gave him a wide berth and muttered their disgust. He collapsed onto his side, gibbering, talking to people who were not there.

A group of loud, drunk men sauntered over, discussing the evening's exploits. One of them noticed Edgar and pointed and laughed, thinking him a fellow reveler who took his celebrating a little too far. One of the other men stopped him and came over for a closer look.

"Poe?" said Edgar's old Army friend Charles. "Mercy sakes, what the hell happened to you?"

Edgar looked up at him, insensible, but grateful to see a familiar face.

"Help me stand him up," Charles asked his mates. "I'm going to take him home to sleep it off."

Looking like death warmed over but recovered enough to leave his friend's care, Edgar skulked through the Boston streets to the train station. Pale, clammy and weak, with a newly visible vein pulsing ominously on the side of his forehead, he unsteadily made his way until a man noticed him and chatted him up.

"Aren't you Poe, the poet? The Raven, Poe?" the man said.

Edgar tried to be polite, but under the circumstances was in no mood for this.

"Yes," he replied, "I am, thank you. But I must be on my way…"

"Listen, I have a daguerreotype studio right here, and it'd be such an honor if you'd pop in for a portrait," the man asked, eyeing the bags under Edgar's eyes and the purple circles beneath them, knowing that he'd make a pretty penny selling photographic evidence of a well-known man of letters looking like hell.

"I'm sorry, I don't think so, I..." Edgar stammered.

"Please, it would be such an honor..." the man said, holding out five dollars.

Edgar mentally debated for a second before accepting the offer and allowing the man to lead him by the arm to his studio.

(26)

Pallid and shaky, Edgar rode a train to Philadelphia. He stepped off the train into the blinding summer sunlight. Walking unsteadily past bright, red, white and blue decorations, Edgar stepped into a doctor's office.

The doctor examined Edgar, noting his shaking hands and his colorless skin.

"I have to be honest with you, Mr. Poe," the doctor said, concerned, "We have a cholera outbreak here right now, so I find your fever and the fact that you're vomiting very alarming."

Edgar's eyes widened at the word "cholera," but he said nothing.

"As a preventative measure, I'm going to prescribe calomel," the doctor said, as he sat down at his desk and measured out a dosage of a chalky substance.

"What's calomel?" Edgar asked, swallowing hard.

"Mercury chloride," replied the doctor. "It's a purgative."

He stood in front of the seated Edgar with a heaping spoonful of it. "Here you are."

Edgar looked up at the doctor, opened his mouth and accepted the medicine, grimacing at its vile taste.

At sunset, he left the doctor's, feeling even worse. He tried to steady himself against a lamppost, but that didn't do the job, so he collapsed onto a park bench. As the sun went down completely, beautiful fireworks lit the sky behind him and the deafening explosions that created them filled the air, startling him. He screamed in terror, leapt up, then fell to his knees and helplessly watched the fireworks fly, one, after the other, after the other.

The fireworks became meteors. He was standing on the porch in Baltimore with Sissy in his arms, who giggled with delight as each meteor flew past. He kissed her forehead, so happy, so content, so in love.

Two policemen picked him up off the ground. They asked him why he was howling and punching the ground with his fists, why they were bloody. Had he been drinking? They hauled him off to Moyamensing Prison and callously threw him into a cell, proclaiming him to be a drunk.

He peered out the barred window of his cell at the moonlit clocktower. The moon morphed into a luminous, silver, angelic female being. Her vibrating light-presence was comforting, until her face morphed into that of a vicious, fanged demon. He screamed, gripped with pure terror.

Next, he was running down the prison hallway. At the end, he saw a light. He went inside to find two blackguards stirring a cauldron of molten metal. One tried to grab him and screaming, he ran away. He stopped, panting, before another doorway. He turned to look inside and there was Muddy! He dashed inside and sobbing, threw his arms around her. Her head rolled off of her shoulders, having been severed cleanly at the neck. He screamed and screamed, inconsolable.

The next morning, he waited his turn in court, pale, trembling and exhausted from his night of hell. After the judge processed a series of drunks and ne'er-do-wells, it was Edgar's turn.

"Name?" asked the judge.

"Edgar Allan Poe, your honor," he replied, hoarsely, weakly.

"Poe? The poet? The Raven, Poe?" the judge asked, quizzically.

"Yes, your honor," Edgar answered, his cheeks burning with embarrassment.

"I wouldn't have expected to find you in my courtroom, Mr. Poe," said the judge. "You may leave, and the usual fine is waived, provided that I never see you here again."

Edgar nodded, shocked but grateful.

"Thank you, your honor," he graciously replied.

Still too sick to travel, with no money and nowhere to go, Edgar walked aimlessly through the streets of Philadelphia until he saw a shingle hanging on the corner of a house, bearing a familiar name: "JOHN SARTAIN, ENGRAVER." He knocked on the door.

"Poe?" Sartain asked quizzically, as he opened the door.

"What are you doing in Philly? What has happened to you?" he continued. "Please, come in."

Exhausted, hungry and thirsty, Edgar stepped inside, sat down hard and began to sob.

"Jesus Christ," Sartain swore in shock. "Stay there, let me get you some water."

Sartain returned with a tall glass of water, which Edgar gratefully gulped down.

"Please tell me you'll stay for supper, Edgar," Sartain gently said, placing his hand on Edgar's shoulder. "You look like you haven't had a decent meal in a long time."

Edgar nodded through his tears.

"Also, Edgar…" Sartain asked, softening his voice further, "Where is your other shoe?"

Edgar looked down, saw that he was indeed wearing only one shoe, and looked helplessly back up at Sartain.

"Jesus," Sartain replied in a compassionate whisper. "Wait right there, you can borrow my slippers."

Bathed, shaved and fed, Edgar lied down on the couch

for the night as John Sartain covered him with a blanket.

Exhausted, he was asleep within seconds. John quietly

pulled three dining chairs over in front of the couch,

making a bed for himself. He lied down there to sleep and

to keep an eye on Edgar.

At the train station, Edgar wistfully said goodbye to his friend.

"Thank you, John," Edgar said, shaking his hand and looking him firmly in the eye so he'd be sure to understand the depth of his gratitude.

"Look, here's ten dollars," John said. "That'll get you a hotel room and a couple decent meals."

Edgar gratefully accepted. He held onto John's hand a little too long. He didn't want to go, but finally he turned and got on the train. John stood and watched the train leave, worried for Edgar.

On the train, Edgar wrote to Muddy.

"My *dear, dear* Mother, —

I have been *so* ill — have had the cholera, or spasms quiet as bad, and can now hardly hold the pen...

The very instant you get this, *come* to me. The joy of seeing you will almost compensate for our sorrows. We can but die together. It is no use to reason with me *now*; I must die. I have no desire to live since I have done "Eureka." I could accomplish nothing more. For your sake it would be sweet to live, but we must die together. You have been all in all to me, darling, ever beloved mother, and dearest, truest friend.

I was never really insane, except on occasions where my heart was touched...

I have been taken to prison once since I came here for spreeing drunk; but *then* I was not. It was about Virginia." **(27)**

Sunset. The man in the lighthouse read the last page of his book, reading with relish, fully absorbed, as Neptune lied dozing at his feet. He closed his book, heaved a deep, satisfied sigh and set the book on his desk: *Eureka: A Prose Poem* by Edgar A. Poe.

He dabbed a tear from his eye, ran his hands through his hair and smiled at Neptune.

"Come on, Neptune. How about a nice walk before bed?" he asked, as Neptune leapt to attention, panting happily. He and Neptune started down the lighthouse's spiral staircase.

Edgar Allan Poe, wearing clothes not his own – a dirty straw hat, dirty gray pants and a worn coat that was too big for him, sat slumped and occasionally twitching, facing the corner of a noisy, rundown Baltimore bar.

"He'll bloody regret this in the morning, that's for bloody sure," laughed a wobbling drunk sailor.

"How much do you suppose he's had?" belched another, equally drunk sailor.

"I don't know, but he's feeling no pain," replied the first.

Two well-dressed businessmen pushed past the loud and smelly crowd.

"Get out of the goddamn way," grunted one.

"Move along, there's nothing to see here. Bloody bastards," growled the other, elbowing his way through to Edgar.

He knelt down and looked at Edgar's face, taking his chin in his hand.

"Jesus Christ," he breathed.

"I told you," said the other. "He's in really, really bad shape."

"His eyes are glassy," said the kneeling man. "Edgar? Edgar?? POE?!" he yelled, slapping at his face, trying to get him to respond.

"This is bad. This is genuinely bad," he said. "I can't take him home. After last time, my wife won't allow it."

"Can we get him a room upstairs?"

"And what, leave him alone there? He'll die. He needs medical attention."

"I'll call a hack. Let's take him to the hospital."

Doctor Moran took Edgar's pulse as he lied limply, lifelessly in a hospital bed. Moran's lips moved as he silently counted the irregular beats of Edgar's heart, a look of concern washing over his face. Edgar's half-lidded eyes were vacant. His hair matted, his skin clammy and pale, his face covered in five days' beard growth, his body shuddered as he listlessly breathed, alive only through what seemed like sheer inertia.

"We walk about, amid the destinies of our world-existence, encompassed by dim but ever present *Memories* of a Destiny more vast — very distant in the by-gone time, and infinitely awful.

We live out a Youth peculiarly haunted by such shadows; yet never mistaking them for dreams. As Memories we *know* them. *During our Youth* the distinction is too clear to deceive us even for a moment." **(28)**

The headboard of the hospital bed rattled loudly as Edgar shook violently and sweated profusely. He sat up and tried to get out of bed. Two nurses ran in and held him down, but he struggled so hard, they had to enlist a third nurse for help. He gave up the fight and docilely lied down, staring blankly at the ceiling.

"So long as this Youth endures, the feeling *that we exist*, is the most natural of all feelings. We understand it *thoroughly*. That there was a period at which we did *not* exist — or, that it might so have happened that we never had existed at all — are the considerations, indeed, which *during this Youth*, we find difficulty in understanding. Why we should *not* exist, is, *up to the epoch of Manhood*, of all queries the most unanswerable. Existence — self-existence — existence from all Time and to all Eternity — seems, up to the epoch of Manhood, a normal and unquestionable condition: — *seems, because it is.*" **(28)**

Edgar trembled, semi-catatonic, alone in his hospital room, lit by moonlight, the shadows of tree branches covering the walls. A single tear rolled down his face as he remained fully conscious, in rebellion against his failing body.

"But now comes the period at which a conventional World-Reason awakens us from the truth of our dream. Doubt, Surprise and Incomprehensibility arrive at the same moment. They say: — 'You live and the time was when you lived not. You have been created. An Intelligence exists greater than your own; and it is only through this Intelligence you live at all.' These things we struggle to comprehend and cannot: — *cannot*, because these things, being untrue, are thus, of necessity, incomprehensible."

"No thinking being lives who, at some luminous point of his life of thought, has not felt himself lost amid the surges of futile efforts at understanding, or believing, that anything exists *greater than his own soul*. The utter impossibility of any one's soul feeling

274

itself inferior to another; the intense, overwhelming dissatisfaction and rebellion at the thought; — these, with the omniprevalent aspirations at perfection, are but the spiritual, coincident with the material, struggles towards the original Unity — are, to my mind at least, a species of proof far surpassing what Man terms demonstration, that no one soul *is* inferior to another — that nothing is, or can be, superior to any one soul — that each soul is, in part, its own God — its own Creator: — in a word, that God — the material *and* spiritual God — *now* exists solely in the diffused Matter and Spirit of the Universe; and that the regathering of this diffused Matter and Spirit will be but the re-constitution of the *purely* Spiritual and Individual God.

In this view, and in this view alone, we comprehend the riddles of Divine Injustice — of Inexorable Fate. In this view alone the existence of Evil becomes intelligible; but in this view it becomes more — it becomes endurable. Our souls no longer rebel at a *Sorrow* which we ourselves have imposed upon ourselves, in furtherance of our own purposes — with a view — if even with a futile view — to the extension of our own *Joy*." **(28)**

"I have spoken of *Memories* that haunt us during our youth. They sometimes pursue us even in our Manhood:- assume gradually less and less indefinite shapes:- now and then speak to us with low voices, saying:

'There was an epoch in the Night of Time, when a still-existent Being existed — one of an absolutely infinite number of similar Beings that people the absolutely infinite domains of the absolutely infinite space. It was not and is not in the power of this Being — any more than it is in your own — to extend, by actual increase, the joy of his Existence; but just as it *is* in your power to expand or to concentrate your pleasures (the absolute amount of happiness remaining always the same) so did and does a similar capability appertain to this Divine Being, who thus passes his Eternity in perpetual variation of Concentrated Self and almost Infinite Self-Diffusion. What you call The Universe of Stars is but his present expansive existence. He now feels his life through an infinity of imperfect pleasures — the partial and pain-intertangled pleasures of those inconceivably numerous things which you designate as his creatures, but which are really but infinite individualizations of Himself.'"

"All these creatures –*all*- those which you term animate, as well as those to whom you deny life for no better reason than that you do not behold it in operation - all these creatures have, in a greater or less degree, a capacity for pleasure and for pain:- *but the general sum of their sensations is precisely that amount of Happiness which appertains by right to the Divine Being when concentrated within Himself.* These creatures are all, too, more or less, and more or less obviously, conscious Intelligences; conscious, first, of a proper identity; conscious, secondly and by faint indeterminate glimpses, of an identity with the Divine Being of whom we speak — of an identity with God. Of the two classes of consciousness, fancy that the former will grow weaker, the latter stronger, during the long succession of ages which must elapse before these myriads of individual Intelligences become blended — when the bright stars become blended — into One." **(28)**

Edgar's chest weakly shuddered as he exhaled his final

breath and the light went out of his eyes.

The man opened the lighthouse door and Neptune slinked out ahead of him. He laughed, so infectious was his dog's unbridled joy and enthusiasm. He stepped out onto the beach and stopped in his tracks, overwhelmed by the beauty of the sunset, the shining water and above it all, a bright sprinkling of stars. Neptune happily splashed in the surf like a puppy, utterly unaware of the bulk of his gigantic Newfoundland frame. The night air smelled so good and in perfect solitude, with no audience to question or judge him, in total freedom, the man took Neptune's cue and did the same, running and splashing and laughing.

And in an instant all things disappeared.

"Think that the sense of individual identity will be gradually merged in the general consciousness — that Man, for example, ceasing imperceptibly to feel himself Man, will at length attain that awfully triumphant epoch when he shall recognize his existence as that of Jehovah. In the meantime bear in mind that all is Life — Life — Life within Life — the less within the greater, and all within the *Spirit Divine.*" **(28)**

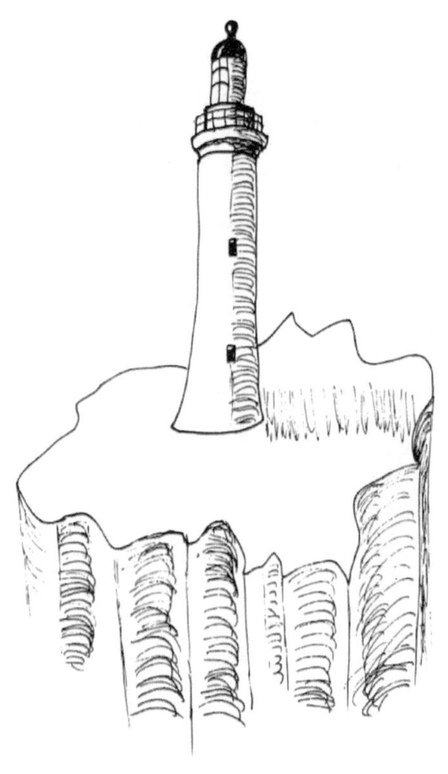

Notes

1. From "Tamerlane" by Edgar Allan Poe, 1827 version.

2. "Enigmatical and Conundrum-ical" by Edgar Allan Poe, 1839.

3. Edgar Allan Poe's August 29, 1835 letter to Maria Clemm and Virginia Clemm.

4. "Eulalie" by Edgar Allan Poe, 1843.

5. Edgar Allan Poe's review of *Norman Leslie* from the *Southern Literary Messenger,* December, 1835.

6. "Enigmatical and Conundrum-ical" by Edgar Allan Poe, 1839.

7. "To be controlled is to be ruined" is a quote from Edgar Allan Poe's January 4, 1848 letter to George W. Eveleth.

8. Paraphrase of a line from Poe's July 4, 1841 letter to Frederick W. Thomas: "To coin one's brain into silver, at the nod of a master, is to my thinking, the hardest task in the world."

9. The Prospectus of the Penn Magazine, by Edgar Allan Poe, 1840.

10. "Long, Long Ago" by Thomas Haynes Bayly, 1833.

11. Paraphrase of a line from Frederick W. Thomas' May 20, 1841 letter to Edgar Allan Poe: "You have on your desk everything in the writing line in apple-pie order, and if you choose to lucubrate in a literary way, why you can lucubrate."

12. Edgar Allan Poe's August 27, 1842 letter to
    Frederick W. Thomas.
13. Edgar Allan Poe's bankruptcy petition, courtesy of
    the National Archives
    (http://todaysdocument.tumblr.com/post/100945836
    306/usnatarchives-october-is-american-archives)
    1842.
14. The Prospectus of the Stylus Magazine, by Edgar
    Allan Poe, 1843.
15. Letter from Jesse E. Dow to Thomas C Clarke,
    March 12, 1843.
16. Edgar Allan Poe's April 7, 1844 letter to Maria
    Clemm.
17. From "The Balloon Hoax" by Edgar Allan Poe,
    1844.
18. From Poe's review of Longfellow's "Ballads and
    Other Poems," *Graham's Magazine,* April 1842.
19. Virginia Poe's Valentine to Edgar Allan Poe,
    February 14, 1846.
20. Poe's June 12, 1846 note to his wife Virginia.
21. From an announcement in the December 15th, 1846
    New York Express.
22. From the *Home Journal* by N.P. Willis, December
    1846.
23. A couplet Poe wrote at the bottom of a manuscript
    of his poem "Eulalie" in 1847.
24. From Poe's January 4, 1848 letter to George W.
    Eveleth.
25. "Annabel Lee" by Edgar Allan Poe, 1849.

26. The "Ultima Thule" daguerreotype, taken four days
    after Poe's November 1848 suicide attempt,
    courtesy of www.eapoe.org .
27. Poe's July 7, 1849 letter to Marie Clemm.
28. The final paragraphs of Edgar Allan Poe's *Eureka:
    A Prose Poem*, 1848.

Cover art, raven drawings and lighthouse drawing
by Sara Wilburn.